the Dublin Revie

number eighty | AUTUMN 2020

GW00401734

EDITOR & PUBLISHER: BRENDAN BARRINGTON
DEPUTY PUBLISHERS: DEANNA ORTIZ & AINGEALA FLANNERY

The Dublin Review, number eighty (Autumn 2020).
Design by Atelier David Smith. Printed by Naas Printing Ltd.

ISBN 978-1-9161337-4-7

SUBMISSIONS: Please go to www.thedublinreview.com and follow the instructions on the 'Submissions' page. Although we encourage electronic submissions, we also accept physical submissions, to The Dublin Review, P.O. Box 7948, Dublin 1, Ireland. We cannot return physical manuscripts, so please do not send a unique or irreplaceable piece of work, and be sure to include your email address for a reply. *The Dublin Review* assumes no responsibility for unsolicited material.

SUBSCRIPTIONS: *The Dublin Review* is published quarterly. A subscription costs €34 / UK£26 per year in Ireland & Northern Ireland, €45 / UK£36 / US$60 per year for the rest of the world. Institutions add €15 / UK£13 / US$20. To subscribe or to order back issues, please use the secure-ordering facility at www.thedublinreview.com. Alternatively, you may send your address and a cheque or Visa/MC data and order details to Subscriptions, The Dublin Review, P.O. Box 7948, Dublin 1, Ireland. Credit-card orders are billed at the euro price. Please indicate if credit-card billing address differs from mailing address. If you have a question regarding an order, please email us at order@thedublinreview.com.

WEBSITE: www.thedublinreview.com

TRADE SALES: *The Dublin Review* is distributed to the trade by Gill & Macmillan Distribution, Hume Avenue, Park West, Dublin 12.

SALES REPRESENTATION: Robert Towers, 2 The Crescent, Monkstown, Co. Dublin, tel +353 1 2806532, fax +353 1 2806020.

The Dublin Review receives financial assistance from the Arts Council.

Contents | *number eighty* | AUTUMN 2020

5   *Stuck-still* JANE LAVELLE

16   *The life within* BRIAN DILLON

32   *Shredded* SORCHA HAMILTON

41   *Last words* LIA MILLS

69   *Outside* CAELAINN BRADLEY

71   *My father's LPs* ARNOLD THOMAS FANNING

95   *Notes on contributors*

Stuck-still

JANE LAVELLE

No longer able to bear the small one's crying, Anna brought the car into a cul-de-sac. Neither of the children had slept well over the past few nights and, in the hope that they would get exhausted and fall asleep on the way home, she had kept them out too late. The cul-de-sac was dead still. As she pulled up to the kerb she could hear the tyres crunching in the virgin snow.

The small one's bottle had disappeared under the driver's seat. Anna squeezed herself sideways in front of his legs, wormed her hand under the seat and managed to retrieve the bottle by balancing on one foot. The bass-heavy music he liked so much, which sometimes sent him to sleep, was still playing, obscenely loud now that the door was open. Figures began to appear at the windows of several of the houses. She offered the small one the bottle, but he pushed it away and went on bellowing out his tiredness.

She fumbled with the buckle on the car seat and eventually managed to release him. She kissed his face, tasting his tears' hot salt, held his head of dark curls against her shoulder and bounced his solid little body gently, in time to the music. She half-closed the car door to keep the freezing air from waking the big one and shielded the small one with her coat. She began to step back and forth to calm him down – gingerly, because she was never quite sure of her centre of gravity these days.

A man emerged from the side door of one of the houses and went to get something from his garage. He gave a curt nod and watched her as he stood waiting for the electronic door to open. Anna kept her eye on him. When he came back out with something small and metal in his hand he paused, as if thinking about coming over, but went back indoors without speaking.

Anna's head was pulsing with dull pain. She looked down at the ragged patch of footprints under her feet, corrupting the streetlit orange carpet of snow. She felt a weary rage rise inside her. She swallowed it.

The small one's bawling died down to a whimper; he fell silent and eventually closed his eyes. Anna placed him gently back into his car seat, plugged his mouth with the bottle, turned up the radio even louder and edged off.

She remembered the nappies just in time and pulled in at the last petrol station before home. The forecourt was floodlit and, where the light reflected off the snow, so bright it could have been daytime. By then the dusty snowflakes were falling almost horizontally and the roof provided scant shelter. Despite the cold there was an unpleasant smell, a bin full of cigarette butts and coffee sludge. The shop was closed except for a tiny hatch adjacent to the till, behind which a tired-looking sales assistant was watching his phone. He shivered in his short-sleeved uniform as he opened the hatch and spoke to her. There were no size five nappies left, only sixes; Anna would have to remember to change the small one again before bed or risk leakage overnight.

She'd left her purse in the car, so she headed back to get it, leaving the sales assistant glumly waiting. While she rummaged for the right card, Anna noticed that the man at the next pump – a taxi driver, middle-aged, with a bushy grey moustache – was watching her as he filled his tank. The small one was beginning to shift. She would need to get moving quickly.

When she got back out, the taxi driver began to approach. Anna hit the automatic lock button on her key fob. He was moving slowly, holding his hands up in front of him, signalling that he was not a threat. He stopped on the far side of her car.

'Money OK?' he called.

She nodded.

'Right you are,' he said. He tipped his head towards her middle and pointed at the children in the back seat. 'You'll have your hands full!'

Anna gave an uneasy half-smile. The taxi driver winked, made a thumbs up and went back to his car. Anna waited until he had begun to pull away before heading back to pay for the nappies. The other day on the bus she'd been sitting side-on to the rest of the passengers, in the seats intended for people with buggies and wheelchairs. Without speaking or even looking at her, an old woman had reached forward and begun stroking Anna's belly. The woman's skin was like garlic paper, the fingertips greasy; there was a thin line of glar under the nails. Anna had gritted her teeth and watched her knuckles turn white on the stanchion.

When she arrived home Michael was already back. He met her at the front door. He looked tired.

'I heard the car,' he said. He genuflected to kiss Anna's belly, then gathered the big one out of her seat and eased her into one half of the double buggy in the hallway. He went back outside and did the same with the small one.

'Does he need a bottle?' he asked. 'I've just sterilized them.'

'No, he'll sleep for a while,' said Anna. She wasn't sure he would, but she couldn't face the possibility of his waking again too soon. 'Can you watch them for ten minutes while I have a shower? Then we'll put them to bed properly.'

'Course I can.'

'How was work?' she said. She imagined Michael at work – standing with his arms folded in front of towers of paper coffee cups, full shelves of crisp packets lined up and shiny, their chests puffed out in beautiful regimentation.

'A pain in the arse,' he said. He rubbed the bridge of his nose. 'The usual bullshit with the wholesaler.'

'Any excitement?'

'Not really. A young fella lifted a few tins of Boost and ran off. I had to deal with the police.'

Anna paused, allowing herself to wonder what she might have done if she'd been there. She imagined herself following the thief out of the shop and giving chase down the street. She would have woven between pedestrians and leapt over bollards. She would have kept going until she caught up behind him and, with a heroic surge of motion, brought him crashing to the ground. She would have bloodied his head on the pavement, pulled his hair and kept him there until the police came. It would have been a consummate experience, his defeat and her victory.

'What happened?'

'He was still on the street when the police turned up. Waiting for the rain to stop. They made him pay for the tins.'

'Right.'

'What kept you out so late anyway?' The sharpness in Michael's voice showed Anna how tired he was. He wouldn't be getting up during the night. She closed her eyes for a moment.

'I thought they might sleep in the car.'

They both looked over towards the buggy, where the small one was just opening his eyes. Michael turned to the sterilizer and released the catch, sending up a burst of steam that rolled out across the beams of the kitchen spotlights. He began to assemble the bottles. Anna squeezed past the buggy and behind it and began to wheel it gently back and forth. But the small one was already shuffling forward. Anna put her hand on his shoulder and kept it there while she manoeuvred herself around the front again. By then he was letting out squawks and in danger of waking the big one. She lifted him out of the buggy and brought him back into the kitchen, bouncing him in her arms.

When he had the bottles all lined up in a row, Michael came over.

'I suppose he's hungry? What will I give him?'

It was the waking groans of the hot-water pipes that dragged Anna from her sleep the next morning. Michael had an early shift and he was taking a shower. She tried to hang on to the last frayed ends of rest when Michael came back to get dressed, while he was padding around the room, opening and closing drawers. When she finally opened her eyes he was tucking in his shirt in front of the mirror on the inside of the wardrobe door, doing up his tie. He always wore a tie to work, even if, like today, he would be mostly on the till. He would skip breakfast, as always; sorting out the hot food was his first task of the morning and he usually treated himself to one of the jambons straight out of the oven. Neither of them spoke. Before he left Michael approached the bed and stroked Anna's arm lightly. Anna reached out the same arm and gave Michael a pat behind the knees.

Today Anna would be at home with the children. The big one was already downstairs. She would be playing with the television remote in the hope of conjuring up cartoons. The small one, who had been coughing throughout the night and waking often, lay in the space Michael had vacated, in a fragile sleep. Anna kissed him on the temple. During the night she had taken his clothes off to keep his temperature down and he was wearing nothing but a nappy and a T-shirt, but he still felt hot. He had the Horrible Ball in his mouth and a sloppy chunk of tongue was sticking out around the side.

The Horrible Ball was the small one's favourite toy. It was hot pink with an acid-house smiley face on one side of the thick rubber surface. The other side was carpeted in flaccid rubber strings, supposed to represent hair, that could be stretched to the length of a child's arm. There was a heavy plastic sphere in the middle that glowed purple and blue when it hit something. The surface of the Horrible Ball was slightly powdery. It left a residue on her fingers that made Anna think of dead skin. It was always very slightly warm – which, since it had no business being warm at all, always took her by surprise. How it kept its shape was a mystery; there must have been some kind of liquid inside. But what made it horrible as far as Anna was concerned was that it felt like a body part, a fleshy, yielding, human body part. An arse or a tit, specifically. She suspected that was why the small one liked it so much.

The big one would be hungry by now. Anna considered how best to get out of bed without waking her son. Her head still ached. She hadn't slept nearly enough. Her whole body felt fragile, breakable, like some antique piece of clockwork. She stretched out the tension behind her right shoulder and reminded herself to use both arms to lift them throughout the day. She wondered if that was what a breakdown would look like – a spasm in the back, a pain so violent that it would halt her body and quash her thoughts altogether. Or would it be gradual, a winding down to silence? She thought of the big one's talking horse, long out of battery, lying topsy-turvy in the toy box with an empty, blissful grin on its face. She hauled herself upwards. As soon as she rose the small one rolled over and seeped into the hot hollow she'd left in the mattress.

She gathered up the bottles and plastic cups containing the dregs of the night's milk, a couple of spoons coated in cough medicine, a few used tissues and baby wipes, and tiptoed downstairs. The big one, having had no success with the television, had taken some paper from the printer in Anna's study and was drawing and singing at her desk: '... in a manger for his bed'. Anna managed to creep past the study door without attracting her attention. She picked up whatever detritus was on the kitchen floor – a lone plastic drumstick, an unlidded tube of hand cream, a coin, a tiny sock – and put them on the kitchen table. There was no designated place for items like these. This was something children did: they unhooked objects from the moorings of their function, even if their function was only to decorate, and in so doing made them meaningless – part of the general, creeping chaos of the space. But, of course, the objects still had to be picked up. As she bent to retrieve another sock (not a match for the first), she caught a glimpse of herself, pinch-faced and squatting, in the reflective oven-door glass.

She put the cups and spoons in the dishwasher, washed the bottles in the sink and sterilized them in the microwave. She measured out some porridge and cooked it in a saucepan with milk – slowly, because the big one was particular when it came to food and Anna wasn't going to take chances with lumps. She measured out the correct dose of multivitamin drops and added them to the porridge, stirring carefully so that no evidence of the orange liquid could be seen. She found the spoon with the ladybird handle (one of the few currently acceptable spoons) and the big one's blue bowl (she might get away with red but had a better chance with blue), assembled the meal and lumbered back to her daughter.

'Here you are, pet,' she said, presenting the porridge. 'But leave it a wee minute, OK? It'll be burny now.'

The big one looked vaguely dismayed and pushed the bowl away.

'No no no. That's not the real one. I want real porridge.'

Anna sighed. 'That is real, pet.'

'No no *noke*! I want *real* porridge. Porridge not cooked.'

Anna considered leaving the bowl somewhere the child could find it when her hunger finally overrode her misgivings. Then she thought about the porridge going cold, congealing. One of them would put a hand or foot in it sooner or later. She took the porridge back to the kitchen, covered it with clingfilm and put it into the fridge. She could microwave it later for the small one. Then she emptied some dry oats into the red bowl, cleaned the cooked porridge off the ladybird spoon, poured out a separate cup of milk and carried the whole lot back to the big one. The big one inspected this new offering.

'*That's* the real one,' she said. '*That's* the porridge.' But she pushed the bowl away again and went back to her drawing. She wouldn't eat it. The oats would end up scattered across the floor. The thought of lugging the hoover up to the study made Anna feel slightly faint. She noticed a mass of grey-green slime emerging from the child's left nostril. She ignored it.

'It's a windmill, Mum,' said the big one, holding up her drawing. 'No wind today. Stuck-still, stuck-still, stuck-stuck … stuck.'

When the small one began to cry, Anna heaved her viscous body back up to the top floor. It was the particular type of cry that meant he had woken up cross – a series of staccato cracks, like faraway gunshots. She could hear a wheeze behind each one, too, which meant he was still unwell.

The small one was sitting upright in the middle of the bed, chewing the Horrible Ball as he discharged his sobs. His face was contorted and blotchy red; there was shit on his thighs and all over the bedclothes. Anna stood still for a moment when she saw this, then turned and went back into the hallway. She felt hot. She leaned over the banister on her elbows, rounded her lips and breathed out.

When she went back into the bedroom, Anna could see that the edges of the child's nappy had leaked on both sides. The shit was liquid, mustardy; the small one had shuffled up to sit on the pillows, then back down to the middle of the bed, and it had spread in a trail behind him. She lifted him off the bed at arms' length, feeling the strength draining out of her body and straight into his. She felt a pang of anger towards the child, then a pang of guilt, and quelled both with another deep breath. When she lifted him down onto the changing mat the smell followed his body and hit her in the face. It was worse than she expected and it caught her off guard. She coughed, covering her nose with the back of her hand.

She eased one of the child's arms out of the sleeve of his T-shirt and tried to take the Horrible Ball from him to release the other. He screamed when she touched the toy, though, and dug his buttery fingers into it. He glared at her, hateful, as if she'd inflicted some gross and sudden injury.

Anna felt the hatred in his look like a blow to her body and a wave of furious protest rose through her. She took hold of the child's wrist with her left hand and wrenched the Horrible Ball from him with her right. She hurled it away as hard as she could, towards the opposite corner of the room. As it flew through the air she thought of the golden dribbles of shit that must be on it, how they would be centrifuging along the rubber hairs, escaping in tiny beads and spangling the walls and the ceiling, the carpet and the bed.

The Horrible Ball hit the wall with a thwack. It just missed a picture in a wooden frame, but the impact was enough to separate the frame from the slender nail that held it up. It dropped to the floor, its glass pane shattering. The ball slumped beside it, smiley face to the corner, blinking purple and blue.

Anna lifted the wailing child into his unslept-in cot. Then she crossed the room and examined the wreckage. The frame's corner join had collapsed where it had rebounded off the skirting board, releasing the broken pane and showering the carpet with glass fragments. There were big fragments, which Anna now assembled into a pile, but there were small ones too, hard to distinguish. There would probably be particles under the bed and along the wall, among the snarled fibres where the big one had pulled up the carpet.

Anna picked up the frame. The picture, an abstract square of dark blue and brown that suggested a tree at night, was intact. One long shard of glass was still attached to the frame, just about. Anna eased a finger underneath it and pulled hard enough to snap it free. She gripped it gently, avoiding the edges, fingers on one flat side, thumb on the other. When she held it up it caught the grey light from the window. The surface reflected the ball of her hand.

Her pyjama top was lying on the bed. She reached for it and wrapped it around the bottom portion of the shard so that she could hold it in her fist. She knelt down on the floor, feeling some of the tiniest pieces embed themselves into the fabric of her jeans. She picked up the Horrible Ball and set it in front of her.

It was harder than she imagined to pierce the surface, and it was only when the shard's point was against the carpet that the rubber finally gave and bounced back towards her slightly. She twisted the shard to make a hole, from which a glob of thick colourless slime escaped. Anna grabbed a bunch of the rubber hairs. Holding them taut, she drew the edge of the glass backwards, towards her own body, until the cut was as long as her hand was wide. Then she dropped the shard and inserted both sets of fingers into the slimy gap. She paused for a moment while the liquid gathered around her nails and in the creases of her knuckles. Then, allowing herself the fevered pleasure of destruction, she tore the Horrible Ball apart.

Anna bathed the small one carefully. Emptying his bowels had restored his mood and he grinned and babbled as she dressed him in a clean vest and dungarees. She took him to the landing. The bedroom door was closed. She would tackle the broken glass soon, but he would have to be settled and occupied first. She set him down in front of the bookcase at the top of the stairs.

'Choose a story, pet,' she said. She lay down on the floor beside him and closed her eyes for a moment. He began to remove books at random and scatter them on the floor. Meanwhile, the big one needed her.

'Mummy! Mum! I want shopping!' she roared. 'I want shopping.' She enumerated using her fingers: 'Keeder, dangen, hooner and deesh. I need keeder, dangen, hooner, deesh and shan! Come on, shopping lady! Get me! Bring me up!'

The pattern on the carpet shimmered in front of Anna's eyes. Her exhaustion felt almost terminal now. She didn't have another flight of stairs in her. Not with the big one on her shoulder. Besides, the small one was standing on her hair.

'I can't at the moment, pet. Not now, pet. Not at the moment, pet. Not now.'

The big one started the ascent on her own. It was dangerous – she had more confidence than stability and, not long ago, had tumbled the full length of the staircase and been black and blue for a week. At this moment, though, Anna would allow the risk. She turned her body towards the small one.

'Give me a hug, pet,' she said. 'A hug.'

The small one bent down towards her, dribbling from his grin, and extended his pink arms. She realized too late that he was heading for her glasses. She wondered, in the split second before they dug into her face, how long it had been since she had clipped his nails. She was responsible for sixty fingernails and toenails – it would soon be eighty – and, God, they grew. He grabbed her glasses along with some of the flesh beneath her left eye, the fill of a fat little fist. Anna cried out. Her left hand clasped the injured eye and the other lashed out upwards in search of a lightning rod to conduct the pain and rage away from the child. The heel of her hand, this time, caught the lock of the stair gate. It hurt. The gate swung open. The big one scampered through.

Anna closed her eyes again. She rolled over onto her side, holding her right hand in her left, and sobbed.

The big one pulled the gate towards her. It clanged shut, latch against strikeplate. She sat down in the crook of Anna's body, leaning her elbows backwards on the balloon of her mother's abdomen, and began to talk to her thumbs.

'Right, boys,' she was saying. 'Cup of tea?'

Anna put her sore hand around the big one's waist and drew her closer. For once the big one didn't object, so Anna buried her face among the soft flannel folds of the big one's pyjamas. She took a warm, deep, washing-powder breath. The small one, reaching for a book from the floor beside her, laid a cool paw on Anna's forearm, so gently she could barely feel it.

Anna opened her eyes. The morning sun was sending a stream of light through the window at the other end of the hall. The stair gate cast a long, barred shadow over the three of them, curled together on the floor, and the baby leapt in her womb.

The life within

BRIAN DILLON

In the summer of 2018, E and I rented a ground-and-first-floor maisonette in Golden Lane Estate, a 1950s development on the north-western perimeter of the City of London. I hadn't lived in a city, not a real city, since leaving Dublin in the mid-1990s; the quirk and calm of a succession of Kentish towns had suited me well, so I thought. Now that I was moving at last to London – the 'wrong' direction in middle age – I thought a lot about space, property and perspective.

The curtains in our first-floor bedroom opened every morning on a sky bristling with forms and colours of mid-century architectural optimism – or, at any rate, ambition. The three main concrete towers of the Barbican Estate, to the south, seemed to have burrowed their way into the blue at dawn, like those giant drilling machines that dig railway tunnels. Seen from Golden Lane, the buildings – which are named Cromwell, Shakespeare and Lauderdale – change colour frequently through the day: blazing now with sunlight, they would blacken against encroaching cloud and turn almost two-dimensional, coming to life again in intricate gold and brown at the touch of sunset. Each tower, triangular in plan, has forty-two storeys, and each apartment a curving concrete balcony, so that the whole thing, from a distance, looks barbed with hooks or claws. The three roofs are confusing, castellated with service structures; at the summit of each tower there is a thin rail behind which I have often imagined myself standing anxiously as if on a cliff edge. Lauderdale is home to a pair of peregrine falcons; it took me almost two years to spot them, circling slowly and screeching, four hundred feet above.

To the right as I looked out the window was the sixteen-storey Great

Arthur House: the only high-rise block at Golden Lane. Once, from a balcony on a lower floor I heard a young man on his phone pronounce confidently to a friend that he had just moved in to a flat in 'a sort of 1960s office block'. At the core of Great Arthur House, which was completed in 1957, is a concrete structure of floors and cross-walls, with eight flats per storey arrayed in modest, partially enclosed courts – not yet 'streets in the sky', as the architects Alison and Peter Smithson (who submitted an unsuccessful proposal for Golden Lane) put it in the same decade. The concrete, rendered and painted in pale grey, shows at the open ends of the sandwich-like building, and in the small balconies attached to each flat. But the rest is curtain walls of glass and metal, the large windows of the flats alternating with rows of bright yellow – also made of glass. Wide yellow cylindrical rubbish chutes run the whole elevation of the building, tucked into the sides, adding a toylike aspect. The exterior of Great Arthur House had been renovated shortly before we took up residence in its shadow. Imagine waking to the sight of it in the late 1950s, when all around was overgrown bomb sites and the tumult of new construction.

I had a notion, in those first days at Golden Lane, to photograph this view each morning: the monumental shapes and shifting tones, a sky almost never without its passing plane or police helicopter. I would make a visual record of what it was like to live with the idea of modernism imprinted in your field of vision: like living with a pyramid or a cathedral spire. But I never enacted my plan, and so as I write the only image I have of the scene is a Polaroid I took during our last week in the flat. A home is not an ideal nor, even in this faded utopian precinct, ever meant to be; ground-level reality distracts from the view, and from its historic conception. Still, I cannot help but feel that for the past two years we have lived in a dream design and locale: the dream at once heroic, damaged, widely envied and despised, almost intact.

*

This version of the dream – perhaps it is a fantasy about home or community – was only ever going to last, for us, a couple of years. We moved out this July. Because of certain accidents of family and relationship history, a precarious writing career and my own inertia, I possess no property: a fact that separates me, aged fifty-one, from most of my friends and professional contemporaries, and connects me to younger generations, for whom owning a home seems genuinely a dream from another century. Related mirage, but grander: the idea that a home, rented or bought, might be more than a private retreat, but some expression of collective vision and even civic benevolence.

Not a homeowner, then, but quite at home, I never tired of that view. Most of the Golden Lane maisonettes have two bedrooms, and from the larger one you come out onto a tiny landing and turn to descend a concrete staircase whose cantilevered steps are mirrored next door, and seem to float in space, only lightly tethered by thin metal banisters. At this side of the apartment, overlooking a pond and fountain, everything conspires to let in a remarkable amount of light. At the bottom of the stairs, a roller blind rises on an expanse of glass that extends the height of the flat: the upper part a large window and the lower a door to the balcony and garden beyond. Door and window are in fact part of the same mechanism, whose lower portion slides upwards in a single motion, carried on what resemble bicycle chains in the frame – like an enormous sash window. A tiny metal label on the frame says 'Quicktho 1928'. The company, based in Wandsworth, made windows for cars, buses and caravans, as well as domestic settings, before and after the Second World War. The choice of aluminium sliding windows at Golden Lane led to serious condensation problems in Great Arthur House, but ours, like the view, were a daily delight.

On the official maps of bomb damage in London that were produced after the war, Golden Lane and environs are all coloured a rich purple, signifying destruction beyond repair. In places there are lozenges of black: buildings levelled entirely. Within a decade or so, passing City workers would see the estate rise to the north-east as they passed through the junction of Goswell Road (NS) and Beech Street (EW); on the map, made by the architect's department of London County Council, there is a thin black circle around this intersection, denoting a direct hit, late in the war, from a V1 flying bomb. What was bombed here, and in neighbouring streets that had been known in the nineteenth century as a vicious and noisome slum? ('Annually it yields its crop of coiners and smashers; it is the recognized headquarters of beggars and cadgers.') To the west, beyond Aldersgate train station, now Barbican tube station, lies Charterhouse Square: Georgian houses on the western edge were flattened in the Blitz, but a medieval abbey to the north, and its additions, remained mostly intact. To the east, the graveyard survived at Bunhill Fields, where you will find Daniel Defoe, John Bunyan and William Blake. In between, by the start of the war, was a density of houses, pubs, markets, breweries, small factories, especially of the textile and clothing industries, and goods sheds for the railway that ran, here briefly overground, to Aldersgate. Much of this area was destroyed by incendiary bombs in a single night, the 29 December 1940.

It is not hard to find photographs online of the aftermath, even narrow your search to look directly across the five acres of what would become Golden Lane Estate, and stare into the void where our apartment now sits. Here is a trio of amateur snapshots taken a couple of years after the war, looking roughly from the middle of Fann Street, which forms the southern edge of the estate. In the first image, the curious fluted-obelisk spire of St Luke's church looms to the north-west above five- or six-storey tenements and the redbrick Baltic Street School (currently the London College of Fashion). In the foreground, a tangle of rusted reinforcing rods, low rubble and a path or narrow road cleared through – but mostly, the place is filled with grass, bracken, thistles, dandelions. In the second photograph you can see the exposed interior wall of a mostly vanished warehouse; in the third, on what had been the narrow conduit of Hot Water Court, the premises, still standing, of M. Rosenberg, purveyor of skirts. This is not the newly ravaged or picturesque London of stock Blitz photographs, still burning and silhouetted with rescue workers, or covered a year later in brilliant fireweed, St. Paul's majestic in the distance. Rather, the ordinary city, wounded and waiting. In an OS map of 1953, many large and small lots around Golden Lane are marked 'Ruins' – but the site of the estate has been left blank.

The previous year, a competition had been organized by the Royal Institute of British Architects to design a new complex of council housing at Golden Lane. Seven years after the war, the population of the City of London stood at only 500, and just fifty of those lived in the immediate vicinity of Aldersgate. Housing, of course, was a postwar priority, but so too was returning the ancient City to political influence: there were hardly any voters left, apart from businesses that elected local councillors. The winner of the Golden Lane competition was Geoffrey Powell, then a lecturer at the Kingston School of Art. Two of his colleagues, Peter Chamberlin and Christoph Bon, had also entered, and the three made a pact that if one of them should win, they would unite and form a new architectural practice to carry out the design. In a photograph of the partners outside their studio in Fulham, Powell is sharply suited with cigarette, the other two in sweaters, a little more bohemian. All were independently wealthy, meaning the practice could produce relatively lavish plans and prospectuses for its projects.

In the drawings that Powell produced for the competition, he imagined thirteen blocks arranged around four distinct courts, with Great Arthur House and its adjacent piazza (today a rather dismal car park) at the centre. In the end there were nine residential buildings, with 554 flats, plus a community centre, workshop and what was then called the 'physical recreation building'. Walk in from Golden Lane today and you'll find a black metal relief map of the estate attached to a wall, with all structures roughly to scale. Looking down: to the west of the tower, an uncompromisingly spare stretch of concrete containing eight large cylindrical ventilation shafts for an underground car park. This court is the main pedestrian route in, and the best place to appreciate the bright, almost Pop presence of Great Arthur House, which is topped with a concrete quiff: the flaring roof of a water tower. The square to the north, including an indoor swimming pool and a gym, encloses tennis courts, originally a bowling green. To the east, one of five blocks of maisonettes looks onto a gated, sunken lawn and a concrete rotunda, with seating inside, that my Pevsner guide to the architecture of the City of London compares to a sheepfold. (It actually recalls the nearby Roman walls, earliest remnants of the old gated City.) And south of this, another sunken garden – the architects took advantage of cellars exposed by bombing – with shallow pond abutting the community centre.

So much for the crude plan – look closer. Like so much architecture of the reconstruction in Britain, Golden Lane Estate owes an awful lot to Le Corbusier, even if it shies away from his most daring schemes and styles: the wide spacing of monumental blocks in his projected *ville radieuse*, the more primitive and organic concrete forms of his late work. But the influence of pre and post-war Corb is there, in structure, materials and detail. Supporting columns or pilotis allow certain parts of the estate – most obviously a low block in black and white, with abundant tiling – to float above ground level, in the manner of the Villa Savoye of 1931. Coloured panels on Great Arthur House and on the maisonette blocks (ours included: a badly faded blue) recall the Unité d'Habitation apartment complex in Marseilles; a roof garden on top of Great Arthur invokes, on a smaller scale, the same building. In the final stages of the estate's development, before it was completed in 1962, Chamberlin, Powell and Bon lined the western edge of the site, along Goswell Road, with an elegant curving block: flats above and double-fronted shops below, open both to street and estate. Its name, Crescent House, conjures Regency terraces at Brighton or Bath, but the building's concrete arches and dark hardwood window frames are shamelessly modelled on Le Corbusier's Maisons Jaoul: a pair of mid-1950s houses in the Paris suburb of Neuilly-sur-Seine. But Crescent House is at present the least attractive block at Golden Lane: something to do with the fussy replication of Corbusian motifs, and the protrusion of messy domestic space above the street.

'Is that concrete all around, or is it in my head?' Golden Lane is not quite Brutalist: a style that takes its name in part from Le Corbusier's use of raw concrete: *béton brut*. The proper term is New Brutalist: first used in public by the Smithsons in 1953, and then popularized by the critic Reyner Banham. Among architects, critics and public alike, the label slipped in usage to imply an element of sheer brutality, whether involving exposed concrete or not. If you were being strict about it you would have to say that at Golden Lane there is too much glass, too much brick, an abundance of cute detail and colour; in places, says my Pevsner, 'the motifs are replicated to excess'. But pause a moment in any of its wind-whipped quadrangles to consider how actually brutal and spare the estate looked when first built, and was meant to look. Photographs from the late 1950s and early 1960s show a complex of amazing severity, almost entirely without landscaping to soften its sharp angles. This is how Powell put it in 1957: 'There is no attempt at the informal in these courts. We regard the whole scheme as urban. We have no desire to make the project look like a garden suburb.' Most British modernism, the architects believed, was in thrall to an essentially Victorian idea of well-spaced green outskirts, a semi-pastoral alternative to the smothering density of the inner city and the supposed vacancy of rural life. There was a mandarin severity in the insistence that city and countryside should instead remain solely themselves and in Powell's aside, in the same article, that he would prefer the flats all to have the same curtains in their windows. But there is also the thrilling audacity of the belief, which itself now seems antique, that dense inner-city living could be, for ordinary working people, an experience at once of privacy, community, technical convenience and constant aesthetic excitement. Not long after E and I moved in, when the evenings had begun to darken and lights come on in the building opposite as we returned from work, we took to calling that block 'The Future'.

We're not alone in our appreciation of such architecture. Barely a week passes at Golden Lane without a fashion shoot or music video interrupting the view. They are almost always amateur affairs: a group of students from the college next door, some aspiring hip-hop or grime artist striking poses and lip-synching to music from his phone, which he has placed on a bench out of shot. Is Golden Lane here meant to signal 'mid-century modernism' or merely 'council estate'? A view across the pond, with its small stands of reeds and its cheap plastic fountain mechanism (both recent replacements), does not seem to communicate either very clearly. Architecture enthusiasts pass through frequently, some of them staring without the slightest shame into kitchens and living rooms. Perhaps they think they are looking into the past. Sometimes the visitors seem more considerate, and we warm to their interest. We'd been there some months when a group of German architecture students congregated on the other side of the pond, while their professor pointed to salient features of our building. When they appeared again on the walkway at the other side of the flat, I invited them in, and they gushed appropriately at all the light, the cantilevered stairs, the ingenuity of the Quicktho engineers.

We were living inside an aesthetic that has also become a fetish of the contemporary middle classes, much as in past decades the moneyed might have wished for a Georgian or Victorian wreck to revive and cherish, or a rural French hovel. At the gift shop of the Barbican Arts Centre, before lockdown, you could choose from a dozen coffee-table books celebrating Brutalism in particular and mid-century modernism in general – among them a handful of volumes about the Barbican itself. (None yet about Golden Lane.) There are of course distinct levels of aspiration: you might buy a

Finnish chair from the 1950s, but only dream of living in a Brutalist building. The renewed admiration of Brutalism seems to have emerged at exactly the time, in Britain, that notable examples of the style were disappearing, or being menaced by government and local councils. About a decade ago, there was a rash of demolitions, in England, of postwar concrete buildings. Some of these were well known, and thought of as mid-century masterpieces or else grim aesthetic warnings from a misguided moment in history. One by one the Brutalist giants fell: the Trinity Square car park in Gateshead (the '*Get Carter* car park'), the Tricorn shopping centre in Plymouth, the municipal library in Birmingham: an extraordinary inverted ziggurat. In London, the Smithsons' Robin Hood Gardens, a vast housing complex at Poplar in the East End, was torn down in 2017 after the failure of a protracted campaign to have it listed and protected. Afterwards, the Victoria and Albert Museum salvaged a three-storey section of the estate and reconstructed it at the Venice Biennale, because something far more complicated was going on than merely the partial obliteration of an architectural style. It was the hasty reassessment of a whole social and political experiment.

'Miss Hayley sees eye to eye with the crane driver, because she lives on the ninth floor of Great Arthur House.' In *Top People*, a short film about the reconstruction of the City made by the Rank Organisation in 1960, Golden Lane is the bright yellow icon of a future that seems undeniable, such is the energy and scale of rebuilding. From the top floor, Mrs. Neville hands tea and biscuits to workers in a gondola suspended outside her window. There are children playing below in the pristine spaces between the blocks, and there's bingo at the community centre. 'The new life will be a good, neighbourly life.' But the dream lasted barely a decade in its pristine form. By the end of the 1960s, tower blocks were being flung up cheaply, prefabricated and thinly clad rather than cast in situ or covered in brick, and quite without the services, shops and community spaces that were integral at Golden Lane. Such buildings were also proving dangerous, most notoriously at Ronan

Point, East London. This twenty-two-storey tower block opened in March 1968; two months later a gas explosion on the eighteenth floor caused an entire corner of the building to collapse, killing four people and injuring seventeen. And a slower destruction was making itself felt: after only a decade, the concrete in Britain's postwar housing was starting to decay. In the early 1970s the building and engineering company Arup carried out tests at Golden Lane and found considerable spalling: concrete was falling off in chunks, revealing steel reinforcement beneath. Much of the estate, including the exposed concrete portions of Great Arthur House, had to be covered with a protective membrane. Similar problems arose across the country, leading in the long term to a perception that raw concrete was not well suited, in the British climate, for large residential buildings – that it was inherently vulnerable, as at Ronan Point, and likely, as it stained or cracked at the surface, to decline cosmetically. The term 'concrete cancer' was coined to describe a small range of chemical and mechanical phenomena, but began to apply simply to the material's largely harmless, but supposedly ugly, ageing. Though modern conservators challenge all of this – both the science and the aesthetics – the hostility has never really gone away.

But the generalized turn in British culture against modernist estates probably had as much to do, even if this was not always admitted, with the people who lived in them as with the way they were designed and built. The estates became synonymous with violence, drugs and vandalism. Interviewed in the 1980s, Peter Smithson complained that at Robin Hood Gardens residents could not decorate the communal areas: any plants or other items placed outside their flats would straight away be stolen or destroyed. It was the result, Smithson said, of a kind of social envy or resentment – a curiously Hobbesian conclusion from an architect whose work is now routinely, in debates about such things, aligned with Britain's brief period of social-democratic optimism. The truth was more complex. Some estates and tower blocks were disastrous from the start: badly situated, badly served with shops or transport, swiftly reserved for council tenants who were troubled or troublesome. Already in the 1970s a relay had been set up in the mind of the British public between modernism, council housing, poverty and other social ills attendant. Outside of city centres where the young or the rich live in apartments, people now mostly aspire to own Victorian houses, either real ones or the contemporary cartoon versions that developers have been supplying for the past few decades: ever more cramped, ever more archaic. Perhaps they always did – most postwar council housing is not really modernist at all.

When Margaret Thatcher passed the Housing Act in 1980, making it much easier for council tenants to buy their homes, 42 per cent of the British population was living in social housing. The figure has fallen to around 10 per cent. Today about half the flats at Golden Lane are privately owned, many of them rented out in turn. On the website The Modern House – an estate agent that deals mostly in extremely tasteful properties built in the last century – a maisonette identical to ours is for sale right now for three quarters of a million pounds. The Modern House will tell you that the estate has long been popular with artists, architects, designers, *creatives*. It is true: half the people we know, or know about, belong to a certain art–media–academic nexus. Most of them own their flats, but some are private renters, like a PhD student of mine who lives in Great Arthur House. Some council tenants have been here for decades, a handful even since the estate was built.

We found ourselves feeling lucky that during the lockdown we did not live in the suburbs, where we imagined life more crowded and fraught. The City seemed populated only by the security guards who stared at us from each vacant lobby, the streets traversed only by a sudden army of runners, like nervous livestock. The area felt, precisely, like a country estate, patrolled by the occasional discreet guardian, into whose quiet courts and gardens we had strayed. And Golden Lane, an enclave inside this demesne. The transient office workers disappeared from the gardens, as did the teenagers on bikes who used to drift in from other estates and hang around the pond, and the drinkers and smokers who sat on the bench in the dark and stared at their phones. Early in the pandemic, some kid decided to spit on us from an upper balcony. But mostly the estate was quiet, and gradually young families, renters likely, and mostly immigrants, appeared in the middle of the day and fed the ducks, or later, when it was allowed, lay on the lawn in small careful groups: a community who'd been hardly visible to us before. Slowly it occurred to me that we seemed to be living in the 1950s, or some version of it that might be imagined in an architect's drawing.

It is easy to be nostalgic about the postwar dispensation that produced Golden Lane. Even at its most aesthetic and vacuous – the coffee table books, The Modern House with its sparse style and matey tone – the Brutalist craze of the last decade contains an element of this genuine longing. The desire is shared by the monied homeowners and the arty renters who could never afford to live in the most coveted estates. We are not exactly gentrifiers – that process was begun thirty years ago at Golden Lane – but rather the gentrification-adjacent, tenants of the first or second wave of buyers, of the Blairite urbanists as well as the older beneficiaries of Thatcher's spiteful, lavish squandering of postwar council housing. We are both extraordinarily privileged and quite excluded; this inheritance of the British welfare state will never belong to us, no matter how much we may feel we belong here.

Over the decades, the bare concrete of the estate has been blurred by both official and wildcat landscaping. The estate's widest expanse of lawn now has a small meadow of wild flowers at one end. A few rose bushes and larger trees have grown where the City wanted them to grow; others have been smuggled in and somehow preserved against bureaucratic intrusion. About thirty years ago, our near-neighbours, Buffy and Fred, planted the tallest of the trees, a birch that is almost three maisonettes tall, in a small patch of earth in their garden, and still disguise the roots with a fake planter – it seems the authorities have turned a blind eye. What they crack down on seems quite random, and cruelly chosen: on the upper floors of Crescent House, older council tenants have been arranging flowerpots outside their doors for years, but have lately found these displays abruptly removed by Corporation staff, on health and safety grounds. As I write, I have just this moment read a social media post about the City's stripping out of the reed beds in the pond because, so it is said, they were not approved when planted two years ago.

We noticed Buffy had suspended a small bird feeder from her tree, and so in the spring we set up our own, much larger and more obvious. I had not yet seen that the estate rules expressly forbid the feeding of wildlife, and make prim mention of 'pigeon mess'; we found a cage to keep the pigeons off, and a sort of metal collar to stop the squirrels from climbing, and before long there were sparrows, blue tits and two pairs of goldfinches outside the window each morning. In high summer a wagtail patrolled about the pond in the afternoon, and for a while a heron had its fill of the fish. A couple of ducks spent their days and some nights in the pond, but when they stopped coming we concluded they must have nested at the Barbican. Somehow over the years, on the green edges of small towns, and always within striking distance of the sea, I had forgotten all about city birds and their routines, their capacity to describe a temporary retreat in sound and space and imagination.

The estate was Grade II listed in 1997, affording it a certain amount of protection from the incessant rebuilding of the City. From the listing entry of Historic England: 'Golden Lane is a unique environment, a self-sufficient "urban village" in which every element of space is accounted for and every detail carefully considered. It has good claim to be the most successful of England's housing developments from the early 1950s.' Sometimes the protection seems limited. There's a good deal of dilapidation about the estate:

wrecked paving, defunct lights, countless scars to the facades of the maisonette blocks: the results of more recent tests of the ageing concrete. The City Corporation recently and unsuccessfully tried to cover the roof of the community centre with mobile phone masts, and they are about to strip out the estate office at the base of Great Arthur House and insert two new tiny apartments. The Corporation considers the estate a natural pedestrian thoroughfare for office workers pouring out of Barbican tube station in the mornings, and seeping back in its direction at lunchtime. It was not unusual, the summer we moved in, to find some guy in shirt and tie basking in our garden, talking loudly on his phone, leaving his litter behind.

At its edges, the place feels besieged. To the north, flats and a new primary school are to be built on the site of the old Richard Cloudesley School, which has first had to come down, noisily. And not without incident: on a Saturday morning in December 2018, the police came banging on our door, and we were evacuated along with the entire estate, when the demolition team hit a gas main into Golden Lane. To the south of the estate, there was once a residential building belonging to the City police (they are distinct from the London Metropolitan Police), a Corbusian block whose concrete alternated with surfaces of black brick and knapped flint: a not uncommon compromise between European modernism and English vernacular. It was torn down shortly before we moved in.

And in its place? A high-rise development of luxury apartments was going up all the time we lived at Golden Lane. It's still unfinished. On our way past, to the shops, E and I never tired of repeating its name in wonder: The Denizen. It sounds like a deliberate affront or joke, a comment on the sheer abjection of the building to come: an ill-proportioned brick farrago hung with oversized balconies, and in front of some of the windows those curious contemporary adornments: sets of metal railings that merely look, from a distance, as though they surround balconies – but there are no balconies there. And at ground level, the illustrated hoardings that surround such sites, with their images of garishly confected luxury. Among the badly simulated scenes fronting onto Golden Lane: a recent James Bond movie showing in a tiny cinema full of babyish beanbag seating; a brown lobby with drinks cabinet, dartboard and games consoles; the sort of dark grey bathroom decor that could only appeal to certain international men of finance. Here, a studio flat in the basement starts at seven hundred and fifty thousand pounds. Having failed to stop the development, which stole their light, some of our neighbours on the estate petitioned to have the Denizen's idiotic name changed – to no avail. Not long before we moved out I noticed a slogan – maybe it had been there all along – on one of the hoardings: 'Discover the life within.' Three months into lockdown, this invitation, or command, seemed a calculated insult to those of us making our one shopping outing of the week or risking our daily bout of government-mandated exercise.

It is August. I intended to write this essay months ago, while we were still living at Golden Lane. But the virus intervened, schedules went to hell, and the anxiety about whether there would be writing still to do in a world ruled by this virus – this anxiety made it nearly impossible to write. Nearly, but we carried on, slower now. Early in the pandemic, there was a lot of talk about the predicament of renters, about rent strikes and amnesties and a stay on landlords' right to evict. At the time of writing, evictions are still banned, but this will change before summer is out. E and I were lucky: the writing work did not go away, our part-time teaching jobs moved quickly (if not easily) online. We would be, will be, fine.

It is August, and the British government, facing the worst recession since the war, is looking to accelerate the construction, or conversion, of new homes. The rules concerning planning permission are being eased, against the advice of architectural associations and housing charities, both convinced that the change will lead to lower standards. Disused office and retail buildings, so this government also says, can be repurposed as accommodation, though all the evidence suggests that such projects too will produce dwellings hardly fit for human habitation – one well publicized instance of the same plan has already involved apartments lacking windows. In the City, E and I have been walking much the same route daily since lockdown began, and now imagine the empty premises of Merrill Lynch and JP Morgan being turned into glass-walled apartments, and the forecourts of high-end chain pubs and restaurants, which usually service City workers, filled with children playing, neighbours chatting, tending to their terrace gardens. I do not think this is what Boris Johnson and his housing minister have in mind.

Shredded

SORCHA HAMILTON

I'll put you in the shredder, she said. And I started to laugh. I'd been trying to get her attention for days, and now this: a glimmer of her old humour. A tiny flash of it at the sides of her mouth. And she was talking to me, which was something.

I looked up but she flicked her eyes away, she wasn't letting me in.

What had I done? Opened the oven door while her cake was in it. It was just a quick open-close, but she must have noticed something was off when the red light clicked, temperature adjustment. Or maybe she heard me. Anyway, she came into the kitchen and there I was standing beside the oven, waiting.

She bent down to look in through the browned window.

The shredder, she said to me, her finger pointing upwards and walking away. Then she was gone again.

A few days before, I'd left the toast to burn to see if it would get her out of bed. Every time the toaster popped I pressed it down again and watched for the smoke. Then the alarm went. I waited, put my hands to my ears, but still she didn't come down. Then I smashed a glass, a big bowl, two mugs. Nothing. Put the volume up as high as it would go and watched one of Dad's old episodes of *Poirot* – the one about the murder in a plane with the poisonous dart.

I don't know why she was baking anyway. She hadn't made a proper dinner for a long, long time – and now? Your father's favourite coffee cake.

My dad liked coffee cake but he died seven months ago. It's been me and Mumso here in the family home ever since. My sisters – I've got five of them – are all way older and married and living far away. They take turns to visit, every few weeks, and observe the state of affairs. How's she *doing*, they'll ask me in half-whispers. How's she *holding up*?

I've made it very clear to all concerned that I have plans to leave ASAP – i.e. the minute I finish school. Two more years and then I'll be off away, I've told them.

Anyway, I don't know what my parents were thinking, having me so late, so I'll let you reach your own conclusions on that one. For as long as I can remember, they slept in separate beds. In the same room but in two singles with purple satin bedcovers. I never thought this was strange until I went to Killian's house. Killian and I were friends for a while when we were younger, but if I saw him now I'd cross the road. Mainly because we both got into his parents' bed that time when I was nine, after I went wandering around his house. We ended up in their king-size, four-poster bed that was more like a ship. I remember running in at it – Holy Cheesus, which is the kind of thing I used to say back then – and throwing myself on it. He watched me from the door and then I called him over. Let's get under, I said. I'd seen something on TV, I'd been wondering about the way people rolled around under the sheets with no clothes, their hands spread, breathing deeply. I wanted to try it.

Take your clothes off, I told him. And he obeyed just like that, he could have said no. Well he was the same age so I'm guessing he had the same curiosities about this whole business. I remember the freckles on his skinny chest and his tight blue underpants. Then he dived under. I'd undressed under the sheets. It was exciting and hot-breathy under there in the white light, the cover pulled over our heads. We lay there, grinning at each other, his arm against mine until we heard keys in the door downstairs. And we both jumped up and started getting dressed.

After that I *really* started wondering why my parents slept in separate beds. I mean, I had a sense that they were different. That they were way older than all the other parents. That my dad had a full head of silver hair. That my mum looked more like a grandmother – in her neat black shoes and the straight skirts to the knee. Most of the other mums wore jeans and hoodies, or high heels and tight working dresses. And she tied her hair up, every day, the same way in a long plait twisted up into a bun.

About a week after Dad died and the funeral was over and my sisters and all the other relatives had gone back to their houses, Mum started sleeping in his bed. I went into her room late one night just to check. There she was, just a small shape under his blankets, facing the wall. I crept over to her empty bed and lay down, listening to the light, steady sound of her breathing in the darkness.

After that, I gradually increased my sleepovers, careful to always come in late and slip out early. And one of the mornings she was facing me across the little avenue between the beds, but still asleep. I watched her, curled to the side and tiny. Was Dad still alive in her dreams? And would she have to realize it all over again when she opened her eyes?

When I came home from school last Wednesday, I found her on the floor. She was lying on her back, her thin hair all loose and messy. I thought she was dead but she turned to look in my direction, then away again. The house looked like it had been burgled, there was stuff all over the place. The books were all pulled off the shelves. Drawers were hanging open, turned over, emptied. There were bits of paper scrunched up and dumped on the table, and all around her empty sweet wrappers and chocolate packets.

Look, she said, sitting up and waving something shiny in the air.

He had them hidden all over the house … she said, high-pitched and croaky. She was in her nightie and I could almost see up in between her legs.

Sweet tooth, Mum said and a sob came up, like a burp, dry and coarse, then was followed by another. I moved towards her, taking large steps over the papers and wrappers and books. I wanted to hug her but she waved me away, the sweet falling from her hand. I picked it up – a toffee in a golden wrapper – and slipped it into my pocket. I stood there for a while, on standby, in case she changed her mind.

Sometimes, way before he got sick, Dad would leave sweets on my pillow. He didn't like me to say thanks or to even mention it. Don't know what you're talking about, he would say, a bit crossly. But I needed him to know that I'd found them – for some reason it seemed essential to let him know. Like I was in on it with him. So I took a different approach, I would say something like: *A strange thing happened to me …* and then I'd have his attention. He would listen up, nodding. Oh yes, tell me, he'd say.

Well, I'd start to explain – usually in a French accent, like Detective Poirot – I heard a sound, like flapping then rustling in the corner of my room, but when I went to investigate, there was nothing there. The sound stopped and it was then that I noticed something glowing on my pillow …

A few days after the tornado – I decided to call it that – the house was tidy again when I came home from school. It was pristine and eerie. Her coffee cake was in the oven and that was when we had our little exchange. I had followed her into the sitting room where she was standing at the table, her hair back to normal and wearing her usual straight skirt and beige cardie.

Look what I got, she said. She was feeding bits of paper into a shiny white shredder. It made a soft mechanical hum.

I'm getting rid of all these unwanted documents, she said. It's the best way to dispose of confidential paperwork. Easy-peasy, she said, and off she went again with another batch. Like a TV ad.

Here, have a go, Mum said, and handed me some old letters. I fed the corner into a machine and she corrected me – you have to do it straight, she said, like she was teaching me something really important. But I got the hang of it. And it was quite satisfying, I have to say, the gentle way the machine sucked the sheet in, urging you on. And then the pages were gone. There was a clear box attached so you could see into the strands of paper coming out the other end. I looked for another sheet but she had them clasped in a bundle in her hand. I better get back to it, she said, and I stepped away.

Later that evening I saw the cake on the kitchen counter, still in its tin, a big crater in the middle. In the sitting room Mum was taking bits of shredded paper out of the back of the machine. There were six filled black bags lined up beside the couch.

It's time you started sleeping in your own bed again, she said, not looking up.

I said nothing, in the doorway. So she'd noticed, after all. Perhaps I'd forgotten to make her bed once or twice?

I mean you're nearly sixteen, she said, putting the box back on the table. Sleeping in your mother's bed. Ha! I mean what would your friends say?

I walked out and went up to my room and lay down on my bed. I may have cried for a bit. Then I remembered the toffee I'd put under the pillow. I took it out and chewed down on it hard. It took a long time to get soft and melty. But it was good. No complaints, Dad.

When I was finished, I smoothed out the wrapper nice and flat and shiny.

The next afternoon when I came home I heard the shredder going again. She was standing feeding more bits of paper into it and the doors of the filing cabinet were open and empty. There was the cover of a hardback book on the floor, I picked it up and all the pages had been ripped out. Some of the frames from the walls were down too – Dad's certificates of achievement, a photo he took of a goat on Achill island. A framed poem about 'keeping your chin up' that he used to quote every now and then.

What happened, I said, but she couldn't hear.

What happened! I shouted.

Just tidying, she said.

But Mum, it's Dad stuff, you can't do that …

She swung around towards me, though she never looked at me any more, more like through my shoulder. Her eyes were red and hazy.

I'll do what I bloody-well like.

And there it was. The code word. The danger sign. Bloody wasn't even a bad word but when my mother used it, it was like an alarm going off. I'd seen the looks, darting from one sister to the next when she'd said it, and I'd followed them out of the room. Let's get out of here, Laura would whisper to me, going down the hallway. It's time to clear the vicinity.

I went into the kitchen and turned the toastie machine on. There were old crusty bits of melted cheese at the side and back but I tried not to think about them.

I should explain that Dad had been sick for quite a while. I know that will make you feel better. Yes, he was sick for a long time, for most of his life, for as long as I could remember. Death, yes. Sad but not tragic. Who said that? I mean, I must have known he was on the way out, right? He was in the hospice for nearly two years. Couldn't talk for most of that time and by the end I'd stopped going to see him so often, maybe only once every two weeks. Sad but not tragic.

Terence Michael Conway 1934–2001

But I will tell you one thing. My clearest memory. Of him putting me on the bike. The tick of the wheels as he approached then stopped to lean it against the wall while we got ready. How he would bend down to zip up my coat, make sure my hat was on securely, then lift me up. And place me on the tiny black seat he had attached to the crossbar, just for me. And arrange my feet, resting either side on a small bar and out of harm's way.

Then he steered us out on to the road and hopped up, swung his leg over and there is the wobble, the quick swerve before we're off. And he's ped-alling hard to keep us right and there's a little bump now, he says, and we go up on the kerb then down again, and through the lights and on towards the sea. Faster, faster and his knee brushes against me once, twice, his two arms either side of me gripping the handlebars. His breathing is fast and full, and I feel as though I am inside his chest.

On the third day of shredding I saw her putting one of his ties in. I noticed the sound changing – the sound of wrong, mechanically speaking. I was making my after-school toastie and popped my head round the door. She was standing over the machine, trying to push the pointy end of a dark red tie into the teeth, then she quickly pulled it back out and the metal squealed. She held it up – in a daze, could she see I was there? The end of the tie was all bunched up and mangled.

I wanted it to be like tassels, she said. I love tassels … I always wanted something with tassels.

She set the tie down on the table and went up the stairs. Came back down seconds later with one of Dad's shirts, then started feeding the end of it into the machine. She shook her head as she pulled it out and again the machine made a screech.

When she went back up the stairs again, I followed her.

From the closet she started to take out the hangers of coats and trousers and shirts. Then emptied the drawers. I sat on her bed and watched as the clothes piled up. I picked up one of his silk handkerchiefs and rubbed it against my face.

Yes, she said pointing to me. Let's try that.

I handed it over.

I picked up a maroon sock with yellow diamonds running to the top. I held it up to her.

Sock? I said, and then it was like a game.

She took the sock from my hand and rubbed the material between thumb and forefinger. A little thick, she said. But we'll give it a try.

Vests?

I tossed one over to her and again she evaluated the texture between her fingers.

She nodded.

And see if there's more handkerchiefs.

And maybe we could cut up the shirts or trousers a bit first? I suggested.

Yes, she said.

We were busy now, we had lots to do. We carried our selection downstairs and got to work, making little piles, cutting up the trousers and bits of shirts into A4 lengths, like the sheets of paper.

I kept a close eye on the sides of her mouth. But I knew I was OK. Her lips were not pursed or cross, just concentrating. This was the first thing we'd done together in ages.

Then she got started, first with the handkerchiefs. I watched as she approached with the light-blue square of cloth, and it disappeared – not a glitch – into the machine. My mother smiled then and glanced up at me. Next? I handed her another handkerchief – he had lots of light-blue ones – and in it floated, easy-peasy. Then another and another.

We moved on to the vests when all the handkerchiefs were gone. The machine stalled briefly then recovered after she flicked the switch off-on. It was going smoothly, now, our little assembly line. The cut-up bits of shirts and trousers flew through until our supply was gone and she was emptying the little clear box for the fourth or fifth time and the smell of burning toastie came to meet us from the kitchen.

I dashed in and pulled out the plug. There was smoke coming from the sides so I picked the whole lot up and ran out the back door with it.

When I came back in, she was standing at the kitchen doorway.

You're a sweetheart, she said, dreamily. Then went back into the shredder.

I followed her in, and she turned to me.

I forget what huge eyes you have, she said. Just like your father. Come here, she said, taking my hand in her two hands. She stroked it up and back, then turned it over and started to examine it between her thumb and forefinger. With her other hand she flicked the shredder back on and steered me towards it.

Mum looked at me then and I saw something glazy like heat in her eyes, something I recognized from a long time ago, from when I was younger, when she used to come up and tuck me into bed. Her mouth was relaxed – a near-smile.

It won't hurt, she said, steering the tip of my baby finger towards the mouth of razors.

It was ticklish to start with, then warm and soft, like my finger was going through a car wash. Then she edged the next one through, and the next, and I could feel her pushing down firmly when it came to my knuckles. The machine shuddered for a moment then relaxed as it continued its way up towards my wrist.

Then a feeling crossed all over my body, as my arm went in, my elbow, my shoulder and it was beautiful, like I was turning into strands of floating magic. And all the while she kept her eyes on me, urging me on. She was starting to smile now with her full happy mouth. And she could see me again, yes, she could really see me now that I was in shreds. Good girl, she was saying.

Last words

LIA MILLS

1

In February 2019, two months to the day after my brother Joe died, a letter arrived. The writing on the envelope was unfamiliar; but my name had been written in my brother's unmistakable, rickety script on a second sealed envelope inside. I could see the effort it had taken for him to form each frilly character.

I took a long breath and carried the envelope to an open window. My husband and I were living in a rented flat in central London, and across the roofs I could see the Victoria Tower of Westminster Palace, where a limp Union Jack drooped the length of the flagpole. Afraid of what the letter might say, I considered not opening it – but of course I did.

Joe had typed the letter on our mother's old typewriter, the one I used when I was a teenager to make out her invoices. (Years later, when I began to write professionally, I bought a similar one in a Salvation Army shop in Texas for twenty dollars.) The letter was dated 2014, which meant that he wrote it after the return of the cancer that would eventually kill him. But the letter didn't mention illness, or mortality. Instead, Joe said that he wanted to explain his decision, fifty years earlier, to join the Royal Air Force. 'I know many people were upset (not least some of you, my sisters) by my decision to join the British Armed Services back in the Sixties,' he wrote. 'The COST to me was two-fold, (including) total severance from you, my Family, for nearly 25 years.'

A family story about Joe goes like this: as a young boy he needed toughening up, so our father brought him up the Dublin Mountains, put him out of the car and told him to find his own way home, a distance of several miles that would have included many long, narrow roads without footpaths. When I think about this story, the image of my brother that comes to mind is from a First Holy Communion photo of a shy little boy in shorts and white socks with awkward knees and a gappy smile, the kind of kid who looks in need of a hug.

My sisters remember a time, years later, when Joe brought them riding at the stables where he worked. Our mother had given him money for their bus fare, but Joe kept the money and made them walk, along a similar route to that of his own famous long walk home.

Here is another story, one he told me only once and when we were alone, which inclines me to believe it – his stories were not always reliable. He told me that when he was small, a nurse came into the room he shared with our older sister and stroked his penis, an experience he remembered with furious disgust. He told me he was angry because our sister did nothing to intervene, although she was only three years older than him and might have been asleep. He thought she should have protected him. The presence of the nurse suggests that the incident happened around the time our next sister was born, which would make Joe four and a half years old. The family was living with our grandmother at the time, and the atmosphere in the house can't have been great. Our father had already been diagnosed with the disease that would disable and ultimately kill him. His mother was hostile to ours, who was finishing the medical training that had been interrupted by her marriage and the war, so that she'd be able to support us all.

Our parents, born in a time of war (1914 and 1916 respectively), grew up in Dublin. The Easter Rising happened on the doorstep of both families: our mother's on Parnell Street, bordering the meat markets and surrounded by tenements; our father's on Merrion Row.

They met as students at University College Dublin and married three months before the Second World War began. Within weeks our father joined the RAF 'for the duration of hostilities'. He was one of some fifteen thousand Irishmen (from both jurisdictions) who volunteered to join the RAF during that war. But our father's time in the RAF was never, ever talked about in our family, not even when we watched those black and white films on the BBC on Sunday afternoons – *The Battle of Britain*, *Reach for the Sky*. My older sisters got the impression that he had been non-combatant, that he taught maths and navigation skills, or was involved in communications.

Our mother followed him through various postings, in England and Northern Ireland, into a world of slogans like 'Careless Talk Costs Lives' and 'Keep Mum, She's Not So Dumb'. She would have had no trouble with that sort of thing. She would never tell us who she was voting for in an election; the only political opinion I ever heard her express was an admiration for Noel Browne. I never heard her pass on a piece of gossip either, or play fast and loose with anyone's reputation. Her belief in doctor–patient confidentiality was absolute; I used to think that if I was to turn up in her hospital as a patient with full-blown amnesia, she'd be reluctant to tell me who I was.

There were six of us. I was the youngest. When our father died I was six years old; Joe, our only brother, was twenty-one. He was as much a mystery to me as any adult is to a child. He had a temper I was afraid of, but he could be disarmingly sweet as well. In a rage one minute, sweet and funny the next. He was the kind of brother who'd tickle you until you cried or wet yourself, whichever came first.

He wanted to be a vet, but he failed his first-year exams. Instead of allowing him to sit repeats, our mother took him out of university on the advice of a family friend, who said he wasn't university material. He may not have been university material, but he would have been a good vet; his love for animals never left him. Later, it might have been a kind of revenge when he told people that he had to leave university and go to work to help his widowed mother support his five sisters. The truth is that near the end of her life, in the grip of a lengthy dementia that made her a danger to herself, our mother was still trying to send him money, escaping her nursing home to go in search of a bank so often that in the end she had to be moved to a locked-door facility.

Joe's connection to Hume Dudgeon's riding school probably started as a summer job, but he went on to become an instructor. He was good-looking and popular. One of our sisters remembers that when the Land Rover from the stables came to school on a Saturday to collect girls who went riding, her schoolmates would hang out the windows to get a look at him and wave.

Because of Joe, I got to spend extra time at Dudgeon's. This was bliss for a child like me. There was always something happening – a class that had to stay in the Indoor School because of heavy rain, accompanied by the roar of water falling on the corrugated iron roof; a series of jumps where proficient riders practised before events; birds minding their own business in the eaves; and pony geeks like me hanging out, hoping to be sent on some errand or other, learning our way around the tack room and the yard, knowing the names of all the ponies, breathing in that intoxicating smell.

After Joe moved on to set up a garage with a friend, I kept going to the stables. Riding-out was the best thing because Dudgeon's had access to so much land, with the Dublin Mountains as a backdrop – we rode alongside the steep green bank of the Stillorgan reservoir and through open fields where the Sandyford Industrial Estate is now. Joe was my golden ticket to other wonders, too. The Spring Show and the Dublin Horse Show happened during the school holidays, and he'd be tasked with bringing me along while our mother was at work. As soon as we got there, he'd slip me money for a drink and tell me to get lost for a couple of hours and not tell anyone I'd been left on my own. I'd hang around the stables and talk to the horses. The habit of bribery spilled over into other areas – on our way to or from somewhere, Joe would stop at a pub where he had mysterious business to transact and leave me in the car, buying my silence with a bag of Tayto or a comic. An atmosphere of trouble surrounded him, to do with driving too fast, staying out late and lacking ambition. To me, he was exciting and alarming in equal measure.

4

One day, he was gone. The official story of his departure was this: He loved horses until they weren't fast enough for him; then his interest switched to cars until they weren't fast enough for him either; after that, only planes would do. When Aer Lingus and the Air Corps turned him down, he opted for the RAF. Later, we wondered if he had been trying, retrospectively, to be less of a disappointment to our parents, trying to follow in our father's footsteps, despite their troubled relationship and our mother's efforts to defend him.

I was nine when he left. Our eldest sister had also gone by then, to America. Within three years our family of eight had been reduced to four sisters and a widowed mother. Joe moved from a predominantly female family to the intensely masculine, institutional world of an RAF Officers' Mess. He would live and work in those surroundings for the next twenty-one years. We all went to England for his passing-out parade, my first time in another country.

When he came home for a break he had changed. His shoes were brightly polished. His accent was different. When he answered the phone he said 'Mills' instead of 'Hello'; and he spoke like a twenty-four-hour clock ('We'll meet at eighteen hundred hours'). The RAF played a key role in managing the 1967 outbreak of foot-and-mouth disease, which involved the slaughter and disposal of thousands of animals, an experience Joe found harrowing. That was the last time he told us directly about the work he did. After the Troubles began, his visits home were rare; and we never knew in advance that he was coming. Once, out for a drink with our sisters, he stood up, muttered something out of the corner of his mouth and disappeared. When he came home the next morning, he said he'd had to go into hiding. Had he really been recognized by dodgy characters in the pub? Was he really a target? Our mother thought so. Our sisters thought it more likely that he'd ditched them for a more entertaining prospect.

I didn't know what to believe. Joe was notoriously evasive about what his actual role was in the RAF, or what he did on a daily basis. He hinted at secret missions. The stories he told, never given any geographical or temporal context, were fantastically dramatic, involving guys being shot down to the left and the right of him while he carried on, alone, to some unspecified objective. If asked where these things had happened or in what context – given that the only war Britain was openly involved in at the time was on our own island and didn't seem to match any of these descriptions – he invoked the Official Secrets Act and clammed up. We assumed that he was bullshitting.

This is what we think is true about Joe's RAF career: he never became a pilot. They made him a navigator, which disappointed him at first until he realized the challenge and skill involved ('Any eejit can fly a plane. It takes skill to guide it to where it needs to go'). A poorly treated ear infection resulted in damage to his eardrums, after which, grounded, he became a loadmaster, supervising the loading and unloading of aircraft. He moved from base to base in England, had at least one posting to Cyprus and at least one to Northern Ireland. He was in the Falklands in 1982. He hinted that he had been in Vietnam, although he wouldn't say it outright and the RAF weren't officially part of that war.

At some point, he stopped coming home. It may have been the case that he wasn't allowed to travel home in those years, servicemen being potential targets, on or off duty. It may even have been that he avoided travelling to Ireland in case it would make him suspect to the men he lived and worked with. Whatever the cause, our only link with him consisted of his letters to and from our mother.

I was fourteen when 1971 turned into 1972. Bomber jackets and army overcoats were the ultimate in cool. You could buy them from stalls in the Dandelion Market, but I had no money. Besides, my father's blue-grey RAF jacket still hung on its rail, in perfectly good nick. One day during those Christmas holidays, I lifted it from its hanger and wore it into town. When I came home, my mother was beside herself. How could I have been so stupid as to go out in public wearing that jacket, at a time when violence was escalating in the North?

I was stunned. Until that moment, I hadn't made a connection between my father's service in the air force during a historical war – about which I still had the most naïve and romantic of views – and the nightly news bulletins that showed British soldiers patrolling streets in the North. A few weeks later, at the end of January, Bloody Sunday changed everything. After Bloody Sunday there was no going back.

Despite our scepticism about Joe's Narrow Escapes, it was easy to accept the necessity for secrecy: we could see its bloody proofs on our TV screens any night of the week. I became so good at not talking about him that friends were astonished when he resurfaced in conversation thirty years later: they hadn't realized I had a brother. At first the secrecy was about protecting him. After Bloody Sunday, it was because I was ashamed of having a brother in the British armed forces. Our sisters didn't all feel that way, but I did.

In 1976, I moved to London to study and work at a hospital. During the two and a half years I lived there, I saw Joe twice. The first occasion was our sister Lyn's wedding. Joe felt like a stranger to me, but at Lyn's urging, I agreed to visit him in the Officers' Mess at Brize Norton. I brought a friend, for backup.

In the bar, Joe introduced me to a couple, having warned me that the man ranked above him and I was to be on my best behaviour.

'What a lovely accent,' the woman remarked when I said hello and lovely to meet you, which was about as far as my best behaviour went in those days. She smiled her approval at my brother. 'But – you speak so well!' she told me, glancing at her husband. She may have thought she was paying me a compliment, as Joe – who had his own reasons for failing to recognize a slur when he encountered one – apparently believed.

When my friend joined us, Joe decided that we weren't dressed appropriately for our surroundings. We were both in denim dungaree dresses (hers was striped) with boots (mine were cowboy, hers platform). At this point he introduced us to a neat young person who may have been about our age but seemed older, or from another time. She was dressed in a navy-blue blouse and pleated skirt, with a single row of pearls around her neck. Memory may have sketched in the necklace in retrospect, but that was the impression she gave: like a nun in mufti, with added pearls. Her hair was bobbed, straight, brown. This vision of correctness and probity was announced as Joe's fiancée; she was to take us off to find proper clothes. She was perfectly nice, and brought us to her room (not much bigger than our guest rooms) to investigate her wardrobe, but it didn't take long to realize that nothing she wore would go anywhere near either of us. I don't remember what we talked about. You might think that an encounter with a brother's fiancée would merit special attention, but I have to tell you that Joe was engaged seven times and was given to complaining that these 'females', the objects of his affection, always kept the ring. We never met four of the women concerned or even heard about them until later; I wouldn't have heard of this one if I hadn't turned up in the Mess. In any case, I don't think his affections were particularly engaged. She didn't eat with us, having a previous commitment. Sitting at the bar, Joe told my friend he'd much rather marry her instead.

My friend and I were boarding-school veterans, and the institutional features of life in an Officers' Mess were immediately apparent to us. We had also worked in a Dublin nightclub together and knew our way around a dance floor. With women in a distinct minority that night, we were in demand despite our inappropriate gear. Later on, Joe threatened to beat up a man I was dancing with – perfectly chastely, may I add. He came and stood between us and challenged this person: 'Are you going to leave my little sister alone or do I have to take you outside and make you?' This unprovoked challenge felt like an act, like something you might read in a bodice-ripper. Joe had been drinking all night and was playing the part of the protective big brother he seemed to think he should be. Instead of the fight he wanted with the other officer, he got one from me. I told him he was being ridiculous

'You don't know that man's reputation,' he blustered. 'He's dangerous.'

'We were *dancing*, Joe. In front of everyone.'

The witnesses may have been the point, for him, but I think now that the important witness was himself. He had fantasies of family and chivalry which he tried to enact whenever he was around us (making up for lost time?), with what must have been bitterly disappointing results. It should be said also that, later that same night, Joe made a more formal proposal to my friend. Would she marry him? She laughed him off.

The next day my friend and I were punished for the giddy carry-on of the night before. Joe took us on a tour of the base that would reveal to me for the first time his actual role in the Air Force: loadmaster. Reader, the hold of a cargo plane is no place for a tall, hungover person of any age to stand, especially in platform boots. Bent to the shape of the plane, we had to listen to Joe explain the importance of route protocols, weight distribution and balance – all while struggling to maintain our own, shoulders hunched, necks stooped to breaking point. He gave us what amounted to an interminable physics lesson, dragging on like the last class before lunch. We were suitably miserable, feet sore from too much dancing, blood rushing to the head as our hair hung down around us, chastened harlots.

5

Soon after coming home from London, I moved in with Simon, who I would later marry. Having a daughter live openly with a man before marriage was not the norm in Dublin at the time but, despite her own personal moral code and passionate Catholicism, my mother took this blow to the family reputation with remarkable calm. In fact, when I moved out of her house she said it was a relief to her that I was going: I'd be Simon's problem from now on.

Having a more or less traditional wedding a year later was a way of making up to her for years of difficulty between us. From her point of view, it was an opportunity to bring the whole family together in Ireland for the first time since our eldest sister left, fifteen years earlier. Joe was to 'give me away', even though we barely knew each other by then. True to form, he wouldn't tell us whether or not he'd be able to come to the wedding, let alone fill the role, until two days beforehand. I was frantic at the thought that he'd arrive in uniform, as he had for Lyn's wedding, and begged him not to, but he kept me guessing about that too until he turned up, the day before the wedding, in civilian clothes. In fact, it's likely that he would have been forbidden to wear his uniform in another jurisdiction, but I didn't know that at the time.

For the sake of tradition and because we were all home, I spent the night before the wedding in our mother's house. She had organized a party. The house was full of people and a fair bit of confusion, as not everyone had realized a wedding was imminent – the party was a last-minute affair, largely due to my reluctance to make any kind of fuss coming into conflict with my mother's determination that a fuss should be made, especially for the returning emigrants.

When Simon arrived at the house that night, he was in a bit of a state, having split the arse of his trousers while getting on to the back of his friend's motorbike. This had the effect of making him walk like a duck all night, trying to conceal the rip. But I'm getting ahead of myself: when Joe opened the door to Simon, I was there beside him to introduce them to each other. I thought there might be trouble, because Simon had been unimpressed by the mind games leading up to Our Big Day. (Would Joe turn up or wouldn't he? Would he insist on wearing his uniform?)

'So,' said my brother, now very much present and in charge of the door, 'you're going to make an honest woman of her, are you?' He showed no inclination to stand out of Simon's way and let him in.

I made some suitably mouthy remark back and dragged Simon past him, into the house. The party went on. People came and went. Later, I was upstairs talking to my sister while Simon and Joe had a knock-kneed conversation in the hall. I thought they were making peace. All of a sudden, Joe declared in a loud voice, '*You're* not going to marry Pipsqueak!' One hand at the base of Simon's neck, one in the small of his back, my brother frog-marched my intended out the front door and slammed it shut behind him. Then he went back to the bar that had been set up in the kitchen, while someone who had seen the whole performance simply opened the door and let Simon back in.

6

Soon after we married, Simon and I went to live in America for ten years. During that decade, I think the only time I saw Joe was in the week after our sister Lyn died. Not, come to think of it, in the two chaotic, grief- and panic-stricken weeks leading up to her death, when we could have used the help. He turned up for her memorial service in London and came home to Dublin for her actual funeral, flying in the plane that held her coffin in its hold, a story he told everyone who would listen and would continue to tell for years.

By the time Simon and I came back to Ireland, in 1990, Joe had completed his 21 years in the RAF, honouring his initial contract with one extension. It must have been hard to leave the structures and protections of an airbase, everything you've known for half as long as you've been alive. He rented a flat over a shop near the base and went to work as a night-time sorter for the Royal Mail nearby. One of our sisters did her best to keep in touch with him by ringing him at work in the sorting office, which irritated him. He left that job, first on sick leave and then permanently, with a disability pension. After that, it became harder and harder to find him. Our mother's dementia, which had first become apparent after Lyn's death, severed the fragile thread of her correspondence with Joe. In the early days he came home once or twice to visit her, but the visits stopped and we soon lost sight of him alto-gether. As our mother's illness progressed, the inevitable crises and vigils were punctuated with efforts to track Joe down. Sometimes the best we could do was leave a message for him at a pub.

He never told us why he had qualified for the disability pension. When he came back into our lives, after our mother's death, it seemed clear to us that he suffered from depression. His outlook and expectations of life were over-whelmingly negative, and over time he withdrew from every interest he'd ever had. (Later we discovered that he was on anti-depressants.) He was also, as is perhaps already apparent, an alcoholic. I came to believe that his exces-sive smoking and drinking were deliberately self-destructive, if not para-suicidal.

7

Our mother died in December 1999. As the end neared, we struggled to find Joe. Eventually we made contact, and he came home a week before she died, and then again for her funeral. His friend Quenton persuaded him to come back again for her month's-mind Mass, and came with him to be sure he saw it through. Q and his wife, Liz, had recently taken over the pub where Joe habitually drank. They looked out for him, making sure he ate at least one meal a day. Liz, who used to be a nurse, administered his eye drops every night because his tremor made it impossible for him to do it himself. Over time, they dragged him into their family circle. After that first Mass, they travelled to Ireland with him every year to mark our mother's anniversary.

This ritual weekend, arranged around a memorial dinner, could be quite an ordeal. Our mother had left Joe money. Q and Liz say it changed him, and not for the better. He bought a flash Jaguar which he loved: powder blue, with vanity plates. The annual anniversary weekend was his other extravagance. He liked to play the part of the generous benefactor. He tipped heavily and ostentatiously and demanded good service – loudly – in return. He paid everyone's fare, from America and from England, and put the out-of-towners up in a local hotel for three nights. He kept a tab at the bar you had to do violence to get around, and insisted on paying for the Saturday-night dinner. Most years my sisters and I would host the other dinners, or sometimes breakfasts on the way up from the ferry, but meals were never the point for Joe, and often he wouldn't even join us at the table.

There was an obligatory trip to the graveyard, which led to exhaustive discussions on the care of the grave. Lengthy sessions in the bar were a hothouse for argument. Even if the rest of us were drinking tea and coffee, Joe would have a Bell's and a chaser on the go. In the years when he was refusing to eat, pretending that whiskey and beer were all the sustenance he needed, he wouldn't join us for the actual dinner until at some point he'd arrive and propose a loud toast, Officers' Mess style, *To absent family*. This performance would usually bring whatever restaurant we were in to silence; it made the rest of us squirm with embarrassment. After the toast he'd go back to the bar. One year, when Q and Liz had managed to reintroduce him to the concept of normal meals, he sat at a different table from the rest of us, eating in conspicuous loneliness, but still rose to his feet for the dreaded toast.

When each weekend ended, he would book rooms for the following year at the hotel reception before he left. Calls to the designated restaurant would start as soon as he got back to Wiltshire, as would calls to us: who would be at the dinner next year, would our children come, would there be partners? The year of the separate table I told him I wouldn't show up for this farce ever again. But I did, the next year and the year after that – every year, despite the moods, scenes, arguments and false representations. There were stark contradictions between the family he imagined us to be and the reality of our disparate, cranky adult selves. The family he wanted no longer existed, if it ever had. We, the survivors, were a sorry disappointment to him. But there was something about his need and his loneliness that kept me coming back, despite his insistence on referring to women and girls as 'females' or his use of a ludicrous, long-outgrown nickname for me that no one else had ever used.

Joe had a habit of visiting local shops when he was home and telling whoever was willing to listen about the death of his sister and his mother. He'd tell funeral stories and was known to weep in the telling. It's probably not to my credit when I say that this infuriated me whenever I heard he'd been at it. We had to live here, dammit, and he was making a holy show of us, long after such displays of grief were credible. Where was he while our mother was ill and why did he make it so hard for us to find him when we needed to, as if we didn't have enough to do?

The Harfletts, Q and Liz's family, cushioned these occasions for us. They are kind, generous, life- and family-loving people. They softened Joe. His relationship with them was real, and weathered many storms. They are far more forgiving and tolerant than I am. As Joe became part of their family, they became part of ours in a sort of osmotic exchange. In the twenty years after our mother died, we saw them several times a year, sometimes in England, sometimes in Ireland. They came to weddings and christenings and hauled Joe along with them. Within their own family they gave him the gift of being part of real, everyday familial life with all its rewards and challenges. As their kids had children of their own, Joe became their 'grumpy-grampy' figure. Thanks to them, he knew the joy of watching small children grow up and had the benefit of their unquestioning affection.

Nevertheless, he kept the idea of us, his family of origin, close to his heart. The first thing he'd do every January was to transcribe our birthdays and anniversaries into his new diary. The cards would arrive a few days early with a large shakily-written warning on the outside 'DO NOT OPEN UNTIL …'. On the day itself he would ring and warble 'Happy Birthday to you …' into the answering machine or your ear. He'd insist on singing all the way to the end, no stopping him. Every Christmas we got presents – the same one for all of us, to avoid any suspicion of favouritism – and a phone call. As soon as the annual anniversary weekend was over, he'd set about planning the next one.

He set so much store by his visits home that they – we – could never live up to his expectations. Having assembled us, he'd brood over us. Were the seats good enough, was the service fast enough, did everyone have a drink? With all that settled, he'd bolt outside for a smoke. My smoking sisters would join him but sometimes he didn't want to be joined and, ignoring them, set off for walks around the car park instead.

Bringing his two families together made him nervous. Sometimes he was jealous because we were all so comfortable with Q and Liz, and he would punish either us or them with moody silences and black looks. He didn't share our enjoyment of the simple pleasure of gathering around a table to enjoy a meal and each other's company. He would have dispensed with eating altogether if he could, while the rest of us liked food rather a lot. Conversation wasn't his thing either and we didn't have interests in common. Which left anecdotes and contested memories, neither of which make for easy communication. Some weekends he would barely speak to anyone.

'How do you put up with him?' I once asked Liz.

'He's not like this at home. He's only ever like this in Ireland.'

By this time Simon's job was based in London, and the two of us would sometimes go down to Wiltshire, where Joe lived close to Q and Liz. We had memorable meals with them – the pub and the hotel were gone but Q is still a fabulous cook – watched countless international rugby matches on TV and had some unforgettable adventures. Q is a member of the Worshipful Company of Plumbers, an old guild that hosts spectacular dinners, events and rituals. At his invitation, we ate in the King's Inns, in a massive hall whose walls were lined with imposing portraits of British statesmen who had had a negative impact on Ireland's history. We ate in the Egyptian Room of the Mansion House. We had a morning tour of two new galleries of the Science Museum, the Linbury and the Winton (the latter designed by Zaha Hadid), led by Fiona Woolf. Joe was not part of these outings, but he came with us when we took the Harfletts out for meals in return, outings which Joe bitterly resisted at first but finally came to accept. This felt like a major milestone in restoring normal relations: to accept the simple principle of reciprocity in hosting things, paying for things. English people love their dogs and bring them everywhere; a feature of these meals was that Joe would go around the room, making sure the dogs had water, having conversations with them (supplying their responses, which often featured comments on the owners beside them), feeding them biscuits from his pocket.

When his flat was burgled, witnessed by neighbours who did nothing to stop it and wouldn't speak to the police, he began to suspect everyone around him of the theft of his medals and a coin collection that had belonged to our grandfather. Not much of a haul, but those items meant something to him. It was Q and Liz who comforted him and told us how badly it affected him. Afterwards, he'd refer to the flat as his prison. It had, actually, been a cramped, stifling environment until the Harfletts renovated it. They made it brighter and more liveable; they saw to repairs when the upstairs neighbour had a leak and Joe's ceiling collapsed. They took him out several times a week, to bring him to medical appointments or to join in their family gatherings. They put us up when we travelled over to visit him, and these occasions added new, genuine memories we could share. My own illness softened me. Joe and the Harfletts came over to be with us during some dark days. From then on Joe and I were easier with each other. We didn't have much in common but we accepted, more or less, who each other was. He stopped calling me Pipsqueak after all that.

In the last few years of his life Joe developed a stammer, but it was peculiar. Like so much else about him, we couldn't be sure how genuine it was. The scary thing was that he seemed to believe in the many personae he enacted and couldn't be shifted from whichever one he inhabited at any given moment. War hero. Downtrodden brother in a house of 'females'. Protective brother-hero. Irishman living in England. Drunken Irishman, *tout court*. He loved to play the successful returning emigrant splashing money and drink around freely – often followed by the sour resentment of a person beset by spongers. The drunken Irishman persona could be read either way – performance, because drink provided the script, but genuine too, because that is what he often was.

He briefly considered moving back to Ireland, but house prices made it impossible. I don't think it would have worked in any case. The persona he had developed in England would have been an obstacle to him here. In any case, England was his home now. People there were used to him and to people like him, semi-institutionalized by military service. For years I believed that, if he came back to live in Ireland or lost the care of the Harfletts, Joe would end up living rough. Every time I heard of the death, on the street or in a doorway, of a person who was homeless, I thought of him.

8

Joe developed COPD – what we used to know as emphysema, the disease that killed our father. It was no surprise to anyone. Sometimes he'd be outside having a smoke and he'd get a coughing fit so severe you'd think he would never catch his breath again – but he smoked fiercely all the way through these fits and beyond. His tremor increased. His handwriting deteriorated. The unusual stammer returned.

When he came back into our lives, there were still traces of the RAF in his well-polished shoes, crisply pressed trousers and shirts in camouflage colours, breast pockets crammed with cards, notebook, small address book, pens. As his illness progressed, though, the smart military bearing gave way; his clothes had to be looser, easier to slip on and off and work around. Finally, he took to tracksuit bottoms and fleeces. He wore badges in support of the British Legion, Help for Heroes, and poppies, not only in November. Unable to shave any more, he grew a moustache and beard I couldn't get used to. More than once, on my way to meet him, my eyes would skid past this stooped, bearded man in his navy tracksuit, inching along on a walker. I'd have to tell myself who he was as my mind refused to recognize his age, his suffering face, his shuffling gait. I never got used to it, his genuine pain. His transformation into a person no one could be angry with or resent or doubt.

Somewhere around 2013 Liz told us that he had been diagnosed with advanced prostate cancer. He had put her in the difficult position of keeping it secret, and designated her as his care person. Liz and Q brought him to his appointments. She went in with him and took notes, interpreted the results, interpreted his responses to those results and generally fought his corner in securing the supports he needed. She now worked as a carer, and she added Joe to the list of people who depended on her for everything. Eventually she came to feel that it would be irresponsible to keep Joe's secret any longer, so she told us, but we couldn't let him know that we knew. If we did, he wouldn't trust her any more and that would leave him alone and vulnerable. As it was, he tried to push both of them away, behaving abominably at times, but they were steadfast friends and put up with it all.

He got a reprieve that time, but in 2016 his cancer came back. From then on, we made a point of visiting Wiltshire more often. I have to admit that in my case I made these journeys more to support Liz than to see Joe, who was still cantankerous but with occasional bursts of sweetness. There were things about him I couldn't stand, such as the way he'd smarm over young waitresses, inviting them to sit on his knee – even though I knew full well that if one of them had agreed he'd have had a stroke out of sheer panic. I'd give out to him, but the waitresses would give me weary smiles and say they were used to him. He tipped them well but in a way that made the whole transaction feel more sleazy. He couldn't bring himself to say the words 'girl' or 'woman' – we were all 'females' to him.

On the other hand: one day I visited him alone. He was asleep when I arrived. I looked through his photograph albums while I waited for him to wake up. When he did, maybe because he was caught off guard, he talked me through the photos, mostly of horses, dogs and people I didn't know. He showed me a picture of a handsome, proud-looking horse called Limerick who had belonged to him. Limerick was kept at a livery stables where Joe used to help out and was sometimes ridden by other people, which was part of Joe's deal with the stables. He brought one of our sisters to meet him once. She told me that she'd been amazed to see how all the horses reacted to him. They recognized his voice and put their heads out over their stable doors, nickering hello. He hadn't lost his touch.

What happened to Limerick was this: there was an ongoing row between riders and a local farmer about whether or not a particular stretch of land was a public right of way. One mucky day, the riders from the livery stables found the farmer's gate locked. They decided to go around it, on a narrow spit of track above a steep valley. Limerick's rider was not experienced and the horse fell, crashing through trees all the way down. It took them hours to get to him. It took him hours to die. His rider had jumped for safety and was unhurt.

And here, for once, was proof. When he had finished telling me about what had happened to his horse, Joe showed me a newspaper cutting, complete with photographs. I wished he'd told me the story sooner. This might have been the most honest, straightforward conversation we ever had. It made me aware of how little I knew about his life. Usually there was no point in asking him anything because he'd retreat behind his personal performative firewall, an amalgam of Boy's Own secret agent and stage Irishman, buying drinks for everyone in the pub. Here, at last, was a real story. I recognized the person he used to be in it. Animal lover, denied his chance to be a vet. A boy who needed to be toughened up for his own good.

9

Joe came over to Dublin in September 2018, three months before he died. He wanted to see his old haunts one last time. He wanted to visit his old school and the graveyard where, year after year, he had brought flowers for his parents and his sister. This time it was fairly certain that he would be the next person to go into it. He wanted to meet the undertakers who would take care of his remains. He was horribly ill and frail. The meeting with the undertakers hit him hard but he went through with it, right down to choosing his own coffin. He took to the bed afterwards. I sat with him. He'd no interest in anything, not even an illicit smoke out on the balcony of his hotel room. I felt a surge of grief watching him say goodbye to the little kids, who hadn't a clue what was going on.

Shortly afterwards Q and Liz found a nursing home for him after an exhaustive search for a place where he would have his own room and be able to go in and out to smoke. The weekend he moved in, we went down to see him. He had a ground-floor corner room with a door that opened out to a strip of grass, with farmland beyond it. You could see the motorway in the distance. A colony of harlequin ladybirds nested high up in the corner where the walls met the ceiling, scores of them, piled up on top of each other, getting ready to hibernate but calling horror films to mind. Liz set out the photos that Joe wanted around him. Pride of place was given to two portraits of his favourite girlfriend, the one he was engaged to twice and very nearly married. There were other photos spread around: Joe in uniform, on horseback, receiving trophies for equitation. His TV was there and his walking stick, and his old-style kerosene lighter, engraved with his initials.

The photos of his ex-girlfriend were unsettling but characteristic. This was a woman he hadn't seen for fifty years, who – as I learned only later – went on to have her own life, marriage and children, and died: all without him knowing. Meanwhile, real-life Liz was there beside him almost twenty-four hours a day, minding him, helping him through every difficult minute with so much love. The photos didn't bother Liz, though. She knew his love for her was genuine. Many times, after he'd been particularly obnoxious, she had said to him, 'You can try to push me away as hard as you like, Joe. I'm not going.'

We visited when we could, but his tolerance for company other than Q and Liz was low. After a very short time, as long as it took to smoke two cigarettes, say, he would need to sleep. He refused further treatment for cancer but he took morphine for pain, via intramuscular injections. They didn't put him on a syringe-driver because he was still getting up to move around, to go in and out of his French door to smoke. He was getting up because he was agitated; if he had been on a constant steady dose he would have been calm. It was a vicious cycle. He told us that he'd had enough, he wanted to go. There was nothing we could do, only wait. Liz was with him nearly all the time now, determined to support him to the end.

The last time I saw him, they were doing building work at the nursing home. The road was a mucky mess, there was a mechanical digger at Joe's window. We could have done without its implications. There was a storm outside, trees flailing. Everything felt turbulent, disturbed; a heavy sensation. All the walls thickening.

'Hello, Joe, it's Lia.' His eyes opened but they were blurred. 'Pipsqueak to you,' I said.

'Happy birthday,' he slurred back.

We sat with him for a while. His left arm and hand were cold, the fingers purple. He had carpet burns from falls. He was skin and bone. He wore the face of a stranger. He faded in and out of sleep but he was restless, his legs going, trying to get up and get out, looking for his cigarettes. Then he asked for one, very clearly. 'I want them. Give me one please.' He sat up and roared at Liz. She said, 'I can't; the doctor says no.' He went back to hunting for his fags, talking about his lighter. He mimed smoking, pulled imaginary tobacco from his lip. He looked for a way to stub out an imaginary cigarette. I cupped my hand, a proxy ashtray, and he availed of it. This was the last thing I could do for a brother I never really had, impersonate an ashtray.

Later, he looked at Liz and said, 'Bastards.' It sounded like the punch line of a story he'd been telling her in his mind.

Later still, he asked: 'What does Mum think?'

Liz: 'She thinks it's a good idea.'

'And Dad?'

'He thinks it's a good idea too.'

His eyes wandered, unfocused. His legs pulled up in spasms. When the pretty young nurse came in he gave her the most beautiful smile and lay back to sleep again, still smiling.

When we were leaving he said, 'Sorry for being such bad company.'

'Sure, we're used to it,' I said.

He looked at me then. Just for an instant, we were both there, seeing each other. I kissed him on the forehead and meant it.

We had to fly home for a few days. I rang the nursing home before we left the flat. They said Joe was sleeping peacefully and should continue to do so. He hadn't eaten for a while, now he had stopped drinking too. But his breathing was regular and he was comfortable. I told them we'd be back on Monday. They doubted he'd still be with us then.

He died in the early hours of Sunday, 16 December, the day before we flew back to London. His Irish funeral six days later was a surprisingly warm occasion, largely due to Q's soliloquy, which was, bar none, the most honest account of the difficulties and rewards of friendship and family life that I have ever heard in that setting. Weeks later, friends still told me how moved they had been by his words.

10

In January 2019 we drove to Wiltshire for Joe's UK memorial service, arranged by Q and Liz. The service was to be in the Catholic church. None of us had been inside it before, and we had no idea whether Joe ever had either. I was to do a reading. Horribly nervous, I checked the lectern and walked around the church to calm down. I had to explain the stations of the cross to a bright eight-year-old Harflett grandchild. Not an easy task, take my word for it.

With no coffin to follow, we fell in behind the standard-bearers instead: British Legion standard and the Union flag and another I didn't recognize and forgot to ask about. We carried items representing Joe – his cloth cap, a photo of him when he was young and hopeful, a wreath of poppies. I carried a framed show-jumping photograph because horses were his great love and because of the years he spent working with equitation teams in the RAF. The fact that the rider in the photo wasn't him seemed weirdly appropriate to the occasion, to his succession of approximate identities.

The priest had a flat, heavy voice. His sermon was about babies being expelled, reluctant, from the womb of their mothers. He lingered on the womb idea. His point was about unknowingness; I got that but even so, the wombiness of it was odd. I managed to read 'An Irish Airman Foresees His Death' without crying. After Q spoke, a bugler played the Last Post.

After he left the RAF, Joe was active in the British Legion and in Help for Heroes. When the remains of military personnel were flown back from war zones to Wootton Basset, just ten miles up the road from where he lived, he would go along to help. As long as he was able to drive, he brought other people with him, anyone who needed a lift. We met some of them in the pub, after the service. There were about 150 people there, and no wonder. Years ago, Joe had left a legendary 500 quid behind the bar to buy drinks for everyone when he died – and told them so. It occurred to me now that, between writing letters to be delivered post-mortem and letting people know there'd be drinks on the house after he'd gone, he had been anticipating his death for a long time. People told us over and over how generous he had been – and how some people used to take advantage of his generosity, not just in the bar. Q and Liz defended him from all that as best they could, for years. It can't have been easy.

11

In March 2019, my sister flew over from Dublin and we went down to Wiltshire again, to go through boxes of Joe's things with Liz. There was his stash of photo albums, images of all those people we didn't know, most of them in uniform. It reminded me of the day he told me about the death of his horse; the day I realized that I knew as little about his real life as he knew of mine. That day he'd told me that he'd run many equitation teams in the RAF. He'd shown me trophies and rosettes. I didn't like the career he chose and couldn't pretend I did, but I was glad that he'd found a way to include his love for horses in it. We didn't want to throw it all away.

There was an album from Cyprus, many images of groups of young people riding horses on a beach. Off-duty service personnel. Out of uniform they could be any group of privileged young people anywhere. Playtime. I wondered how people in Cyprus felt about their presence. Lyn's husband was a Cypriot, and it was strange to think of her in-laws a few miles up the road, the completely different worlds they inhabited. No stranger than thinking about him being posted to Northern Ireland, to do god knows what, without our knowing he was there.

12

A few months later, we headed out early for the RAF museum in Hendon – which turned out to be in Colindale, within a mile of Lyn's old home, where I used to spend weekends with her and Adam back in the 1970s. It was almost exactly eighty years to the day since our father got his commissioning scroll.

So many circles closing.

We'd been in touch to ask if the museum would be interested in Joe's albums and certificates. The curator I'd corresponded with was nice, interested. He asked about Joe and if there had been trouble in the family because he joined the RAF. No one had ever asked me this before. I answered as honestly as I could. The curator took most of the things we'd brought. I was relieved. He turned down Joe's serious-looking knives because they were not RAF issue. He advised us to turn them in at a police station. He wavered about the navigation tools but then said they could be useful in a teaching/hands-on situation for kids. They didn't have much material on equitation, so he was happy to get it.

13

The first anniversary of Joe's death was on the day before our mother's twentieth – which also marked his return to our lives. Twenty years of ambivalence, awkwardness, pity, rage and stubborn affection. The Harfletts came over for the weekend. If Q and Liz hadn't come into his life, and ours, who knows what those twenty years would have been like. They were his friends, his family, his caretakers and guardians. It was they who, acting on the instructions of his will, retrieved the letters Joe wrote to us in 2013 and sent them on to us.

That letter – we all got the same one – opened with a rambling apology for having typed it, because his handwriting had become illegible. It was absolutely characteristic of him to focus on something irrelevant in a poor-mouth sort of way, in order to avoid saying the real, true, difficult thing, which was that he knew his condition was terminal and there were things he wanted to say to us, his sisters, before he died. Liz had told us of the existence of these letters but none of us knew what they would say; we couldn't ask him about them because we weren't supposed to know. So we did what you do with things you're not supposed to know: we forgot about them. Well, I did. Joe's letter, when it came, took me by surprise.

It contained no dark confession, no plea for forgiveness, only a tortuous explanation for his decision to join the RAF in 1967. He said he did it because of the Cold War. Wanting to protect us, his sisters, and our free and democratic way of life, he had to choose whether he would enlist with the Americans or with the British. He chose the British. He said he did it so that we would be safe. This melodramatic rationalization didn't ring true with any of us, although the preoccupation with an ideal of protection was at least consistent.

He also wanted us to understand why he never had a family of his own. 'Because of previous experience of having to deal with Families in distress and because I did not expect to survive to the end of my contract, I determined I would not get too close to, or permit any girl to get too close to me, so she would be spared the worry, tension and grief I had seen (and would see a lot more in the future) wives, girlfriends and families experience in the past. This decision would have an adverse effect on me when I eventually retired.'

But it didn't stop the serial engagements. Joe was only forty-five years old when he left the air force. He had time to build relationships, form a family of his own, if he wanted to. That he didn't do it is somehow characteristic, as if, in his depression, he made conscious decisions to sabotage his own happiness. After his horse Limerick was killed, he stopped going to the livery stables. He could have continued helping out, riding other people's horses – but no. He deprived himself of that pleasure and of the companionship of people who shared his interest. Similarly, when his last dog, Harry, died (also of cancer, during which illness Joe brought him for acupuncture every week) he said he wouldn't get another dog because it wouldn't be fair to the animal when he, Joe, died. Again, he deprived himself of a valuable, loving, *real* relationship so as not to inflict pain on the beloved when he died. I think it's fair to say that everyone in our family grew up in the shadow and expectation of death, which has haunted us in different ways; but Joe outlived his last dog by twenty years, and would have outlived at least one more. The story he told himself and us about his life was one long series of renunciations for noble, even sacrificial, reasons – reasons that had little basis in reality.

His letter said that he became anti-social and stayed away from us because he found it difficult to be around our expanding families, because he saw what he had missed and it made him jealous. That word, jealous, grabbed me by the throat. It seemed to be the one true word he wrote. It was a huge, brave admission. If he had been able to say it while he was alive, what difference might it have made? Maybe none, but it might at least have shifted us gently towards the ground of a genuine relationship.

I have often wondered how hard it must have been to be an Irishman in the British armed forces during the seventies and eighties, with the Troubles in full swing, on top of the good old-fashioned anti-Irish sentiment that is so ingrained in British institutions. When I tried to ask, he would only make gestures to signify *I can't talk about this* and head to the bar, or go outside for a smoke. Asked if he'd regretted his decision when the Troubles began, he seemed genuinely surprised. No, of course not. They were there to keep the peace. He said his loyalty was to his men.

I was overwhelmed by the fact of Joe's letter, but infuriated, too, by the wasted opportunity it represented. Even as his loneliness seeped off the page into my heart, even as part of me recognized that he wanted us to think well of him, to know that he loved us in his own way and to part on good terms, I didn't believe him. He was doing what he always did: whitewashing the past and his inflated view, not of our actual family or his real, chosen family (the Harfletts), but of an abstract, idealized 'Family'. There was nothing in his letter that he couldn't have said to us face to face, but if he had we would have been able to question, to argue – and we would have. We're an argumentative lot.

A mean part of me couldn't help feeling that what Joe's letter was really about was having the last, unanswerable, word; telling one last whopper and hoping he'd get away with it. If I was a more generous person I'd let it lie.

Outside

CAELAINN BRADLEY

I sleep with a lot of different men because I like seeing the insides of their houses. There are other reasons, of course, the kind I could dissect at length with a therapist if that weekly hour spent discussing myself was a luxury I could afford any more. But those other reasons are complicated, and this one is simple.

The accountant lived in a small but luxurious apartment in the city centre. I liked to turn the dimmers up and down, to lie on his leather sofa and watch the widescreen TV. He left me there once while he went to work and I took a long, long bath, soaking until my fingers wrinkled. Afterwards I walked around in his robe, drinking his coffee and eating his bagels, nosing through his bookshelves, hoping he wouldn't come back on his lunch break.

The teacher rented a small room in a terraced redbrick by a railway station. Trains rattled past loudly, but inside every surface was covered in houseplants and a golden lamp turned the room a soft yellow. I lay on his bed in the dark, curtains open, watching the city glitter outside. He told me one of his housemates had noisy sex every Monday and Thursday, between 9 and 10 p.m. I wanted to know who with; and why so scheduled? Was he having an affair, perhaps with a yoga-pants-wearing working mother who could manage only those hours? The teacher didn't know. He didn't talk to his roommates. He told me how he hated living there, how he only did it for the low rent, how he mostly stayed in his room and watched TV. He told me, laughingly, that I would have to come over some Monday or Thursday and hear for myself. I laughed along, but I only stayed in the teacher's that one night, and afterwards stopped answering his calls.

The architect is twice my age and owns an ivy-covered house in Ranelagh.

With a grandfather clock in the hall, and a modern kitchen done in elegant greys, and dark wooden floorboards that creak beneath my feet.

The architect talks about his ex-wife a lot. The affairs she had, the furniture she broke, the letter in which she informed him she was gone to Spain and wouldn't be coming back. She was an artist. His mouth twists at the corner as he tells me she cared more about painting than she ever did about him.

He still keeps a photo of her above the fireplace. She is beautiful in that late-forties way, with soft crow's feet and a long graceful neck. The last he heard, the architect tells me, mouth twisting again, she was living with a film director in the mountains outside Granada.

I picture their house, the architect's artist ex-wife and her film director's. A view of the snow-tipped mountains, perhaps, her paintings on the walls, spacious rooms filled with light, a wooden breakfast table where they eat marmalade with fresh crusty bread and discuss films.

While the architect sleeps in, I make coffee, sit at his marble island in a patch of sunlight, and pretend this kitchen is mine. All the grey and glass. The *Sunday Times* and the *New Yorker* on the glossy countertop.

I'm too embarrassed to ask the architect for bus fare, so I walk home. I have €1.20 exactly, and when I reach Grand Canal Basin I spend it on a small bottle of chocolate milk and sit on a bench.

There's an abandoned boat on the water's edge on the other side of the basin. The summer before last, at the tail end of a night out, me and two friends climbed up on that boat. We watched the sunrise, and played music on a portable speaker, and ate pastries we'd stolen from a 24-hour Tesco. I remember feeling good about everything: the sky, the stale pastries, the people beside me. I just don't remember how.

I drink my chocolate milk, and watch the seagulls, and wonder how I'm going to get back inside my life. Then I put the empty bottle in a bin and continue to walk. I've done this walk before. I've another half an hour to go before I'm home.

My father's LPs

ARNOLD THOMAS FANNING

About three years ago, my sister needed to clear out her attic. She had been storing my father's collection of LPs there, and I offered to take the lot of them.

For a long time after my father's death, in 2005, I had felt physically uneasy handling those of his possessions that I'd inherited: his books and his wristwatch, for example; some things more than others. This reflected my own unease in my relationship with him, an anger that stemmed from what I had long perceived to be his coldness towards me. After years of psycho-analysis, however, and through writing about my past and this relationship, I managed to release the bitterness that had been tormenting me, and I felt at ease handling the things that had once been his. So it was that, at the time I received his LPs from my sister, I was wearing his wristwatch and reading his poetry books.

The collection consisted of about 120 long-play 33 1/3 r.p.m. discs. They were originally acquired in a period from the 1950s to the 1980s. I was pre-sent at the purchase of some of them, during the weekly grocery shop, which we went on as a family together, in a small music store on the ground floor of the Dún Laoghaire Shopping Centre, which was then new. A price tag on one of the albums, dating from 1979, reads: 'Murray's Record Centre, 71 Upper George's Street, Dún Laoghaire', with the price marked in punts at £1.99. Many of the records are in Golden Discs sleeves, and I assume that my father acquired these on sorties into Dublin city centre.

As a child I asked my father, 'What kind of music do people listen to as they get older?' To which my father replied: 'They don't buy records any more because they are up to their eyes in debt.' I remember hoping that wasn't true; there seemed so much music still to acquire, still to listen to.

To listen to the records, I bought a cheap box-style turntable and connected it with a cable to my old midi stereo system console and then to two 60-watt speakers, using the stereo as an amplifier to get the best sound I could.

1

Franz Schubert: 'Margaret Price Sings Schubert Lieder': James Lockhart, Piano, and Jack Brymer, Clarinet. EMI Classics for pleasure, CFP166 (1971).

'When in doubt, release the trout,' my father said whenever he played this recording, which includes Schubert's popular tune 'Die Forelle' ('The Trout'). He was referring to the practice of using this most evergreen of tunes in advertising: when stuck for ideas, use an old reliable.

My father was an advertising man. From comments he made over the years, I understood that he did not rate this line of work very highly in the grander scheme of things. He had been to art college briefly, and was a life-long amateur painter; perhaps he'd have been happier working in graphic design. Once, telling me how his day had gone, he recounted a marketing meeting with a petrol company. He and the company executives had been discussing a prize giveaway the company was running as a promotion. One of the prizes was a large fluffy toy in the shape of a caterpillar, coloured pink. There was a question over the number of legs the toy had, and this needed to be accurate for the advertising copy. This led to much animated discussion, before the toy itself was brought to the executives' table and its legs counted.

'Imagine,' my father said, both in horror at his role in this farce and glee at how ridiculous it all was, 'a group of grown men counting the legs of a fluffy caterpillar.' He made it sound like just one more funny thing he had to endure as the advertising executive he was, as opposed to the artist I think he felt himself to be; but underlying it was a sense of the indignity of it all.

There were many benefits, however, to my father's work. He had the Phillips account, for example, and would get discounts or samples of their products from time to time; so it was we had a Phillips vacuum cleaner, radio, and stereo amplifier, amongst other things. He had the Cadbury account, so he would frequently arrive home with boxes of chocolates, making me popular with the neighbourhood kids. And he was the lead executive promoting Sam Spudz, a new brand of potato crisp, uniquely, for its time (the late '70s), 'crinkled', and so he would bring back boxes and boxes of samples.

Around this time, when I was nine or ten, my father and his colleagues commandeered me to assist in a pitch for Sam Spudz. New ideas would have to be presented to the company reps before the go-ahead for a campaign could be granted; on this occasion, I was to be part of the presentation .

My father worked strictly nine to five, Monday to Friday, so it was unusual when, on a weekend morning, he and I went to his office in a Georgian building in Fitzwilliam Street, empty of its regular staff, where a simple film studio had been set up in the basement. The script and set-up were simple: I was filmed eating a Sam Spudz crisp, and dialogue was added in voiceover to the soundtrack. Afterwards, my father and I and the director and technicians watched the video:

> Close-up: A Sam Spudz crinkled crisp.
> Voiceover: 'This is a Sam Spudz crinkled crisp.'
> Cut to: A hand appears and whisks the crisp away.
> Cut to: My face, in agonizing close-up, chewing vigorously, and with large gestures, what the viewer can assume is the crisp.
> Voiceover (*world-weary*): 'That *was* a Sam Spudz crinkled crisp.'

Nothing ever came of that ad, as far as I know; certainly I never saw it broadcast. Maybe it was turned down by the Sam Spudz execs. Maybe it never even got to the point of being presented to them. My own experience of the filming was of becoming increasingly self-conscious, take after take, about that unforgiving close-up of my face chewing, and of the lurid redness of my lips, which I could see on the monitor and which I tried to disguise, to no avail, by sucking them between my teeth.

Back then, I assumed my father had used me for the filming out of expediency, and I resented his taking this short cut which only ended up making me feel embarrassed. Now I think of it differently, and wonder whether he considered it a treat for me, an adventure, to come to the office for filming – something that should have been exciting for a child, and an opportunity, on his part, to show me off to his colleagues.

'This is my son, of whom I am most proud,' my father would sometimes say, quoting the King James Bible that his mother, a Presbyterian, had inspired him to read and carry with him when he went to Mass. He'd say it when others complimented me; I always felt unsure if he was referring to me or to some biblical figure, but now I see it was me he was referring to, that it was his way of complimenting me.

Margaret Price Sings Schubert Lieder was one of the Classics for Pleasure series put out by EMI, of which my father had several in his collection. In the liner notes Leo Black writes on Schubert and of the dozen Lieder here collected: 'His achievement is supreme and likely always to remain so.' Of Margaret Price he says: 'This is her first record of Schubert Lieder and we are proud to be able to present such a superb performance.'

This is stately, elegant, ornate music, the voice fluid and piercing over the insistent piano, and utterly, timelessly beautiful. I can still bring to mind the pause my father took, just as he was about to place this record on the turntable, to utter the phrase: 'When in doubt, release the trout.'

2

Johannes Brahms: Violin Sonatas Nos 1-3; César Franck: Violin Sonata in A: Anne-Sophie Mutter; Alexis Weissenberg. EMI Records Ltd, 2LP set, SLS 143433 (1983).

Some tunes remain in my mind from adolescence; certain phrases, lilts of melody, echoes of harmony. I might not be able to name or identify or fully recall these pieces of music, but once heard again they become present in consciousness as if never absent: permanent, indelible.

One such is the opening phrase of Brahms's Violin Sonata No. 1 in G, Opus 78. A gently distant piano leads into the yearning, almost pleading melody played on the violin which it accompanies; what follows is a piece that transports me completely and utterly to the past.

The recording of this piece in my father's collection is a 1983 LP with Anne-Sophie Mutter on violin and Alexis Weissenberg on piano. In 1983 I was fourteen, unhappy at school, a sulky adolescent dissatisfied with many aspects of his life. The music evokes autumn, my favourite season, evenings drawing in, the air growing cooler, and the living room of the suburban south Dublin house I grew up in being prepared for upcoming winter. No longer would the door that led from the living room to the patio in the back garden be left open all day long, and all evening too, as it had been during the summer. Rather it would be sealed, as would the seams of the windows, with strips of brown masking tape, the type my father acquired in large quantities from his office and used in his art.

The fire would be prepared and sometimes the chimney sweep would be called in to give the chimney a thorough clean before the fire was brought back into service for the colder months. A supply of coal was ordered; the coalman had a ridiculously apt name (I remember it as 'Mr Black'), source of much merriment in our household, and he would be booked to make a delivery. This he did in a flatbed truck that pulled up outside our house, and Mr

Black and his crew of minions, all covered head to toe in coal dust, would bring the coal through the house in large bags hoisted over their shoulders, down the hall, through the kitchen, out the side door through the garage conversion, there to open the bags and deposit the coal with a loud clatter in the bunker made of cinder blocks my father had built especially to store it.

The coalmen never went around the side of the house via the garden to deliver the coal, which would have been cleaner; rather they wanted the shortest route from the front, which meant a lot of hoovering after. The coal, then, was emptied with an explosive rumble from hessian sacks onto the floor of the concrete bunker; the empty sacks would be piled up in the yard and counted to calculate the price that Mr Black quoted to my mother.

Now we had a supply of coal laid in, the glistening black pile visible from the kitchen window.

In the evening, the fire would be cleared of any spent ash by my father; he'd gather it into thick folds of old newspaper and remove it to the coal scuttle, a thick plastic bucket utilized for this purpose, outside. The fire would be set with firelighters and coal only – I do not recall kindling ever being used – and it would be lit early in the evening. Within a few hours it would be at full roar, and we would all be glowing before it.

On the rug immediately in front of the fireplace, my dog, black and lanky, would spread herself out until my father banished her to her own corner of the room. Often, indignant at this disturbance, she would use this moment, yawning and eyeing my father warily, to attempt to climb onto the sofa beside me, where I sat reading. This insolence would also be rebuffed by my father, with a clap of his hands and a shout of 'Out, out,' that made the dog react in alarm and move away, visibly miffed that her dignity and privilege were being called into question.

This was an opportunity for the cat to take the dog's place on the rug by the fire; she was allowed to remain where she lay in front of the roaring coals, growing hotter and hotter as the evening progressed, purring furiously in pleasure as she did so, and directing occasional smirking glances at the dog that seemed to affirm her superior position in the household's hierarchy.

This, the hottest part of the evening, the fire at full throttle, was after dinner. By now, homework done, dishes washed, perhaps even the TV done with for the day, books out, the members of the family – my father, my mother, my sister, and myself – on our various perches reading, animals in their rightful places, the day would wind down: but there was still time for my father to select a record.

To ease himself from where he sat comfortably in his armchair by the fire, he'd first tug at his trousers to create some give in the leg, stretch his arms out before himself for balance as if performing a physical or acrobatic exercise, and ascend slowly, so as to avoid a head-rush.

The records were kept in a long sideboard, a huge thing of dark brown stained wood, with drawers on one end full of bric-a-brac, my mother's sewing things, and two sections of my father's cassettes of homemade recordings from the radio; a large mid-section which contained the drinks cabinet, bottles of A Winter's Tale sherry, Blue Nun and Black Tower and Mateus wines, various ports, whiskies, gins, small bottles of Club mixers, and endless packets of dry-roasted peanuts my father had got from a company he promoted; also there was the good china, a large matching set in blue which was a present to my mother from my father on the occasion of a significant wedding anniversary; and finally the section at the end, with a single door that opened with a hinge that gave a faintly audible hiss, which was dedicated to my father's very slowly growing LP collection.

This end of the cabinet was just beside the spot where I often sat at the dining table completing my Airfix models or drawing or making airplanes out of balsa wood; I could therefore closely observe my father hunkering down to the bureau, as he took time to consider which record to select that evening.

My father was a thin man of average height, with dark hair, brown eyes deeply set under a strong brow, and a prominent nose and chin. Despite his short stature he managed to move in a rangy, lanky manner, to fold himself or stoop as if from a height to address himself to a task, such as, now, picking out a record. Eventually it was decided, the sideboard door gently closed, the record brought to the far end of the living-room.

My father's sound system when I was a child consisted of a turntable, combined amplifier with tape deck and radio, and speakers. The amp was the Phillips, of course, but the turntable was a Sony, and it was silver, unlike the other components which had a faux-wooden veneer.

My father, then, lifting the clear plastic lid of the turntable, slipping the LP carefully in its paper inner sleeve out of its cover into his hand, holding the record gingerly between thumb and fingertips, laying the album gently onto the turntable platter, cleaning the record with a damp cloth, cleaning the stylus with its brush, switching on the turntable, moving the tone arm into position over the first groove, lowering the arm down into place with its lever, standing back a moment at the first hiss of sound coming through the speakers; then, as the music began, adjusting the balance and finally, satisfied, returning to his chair.

The music begins, and it is the Brahms Violin Sonata No. 1. I could not have identified it as such back then if asked to do so, but that gentle piano leading into the more insistent yet tender violin was familiar to me, a melody I loved even at that age, in my mid-adolescence, and that can still take me back to the sensations of the home in which I first heard it played.

3

Stephen Foster: 'Songs of Stephen Foster': John De Gaetani, Mezzo-Soprano;
Leslie Quinn, Baritone; Gilbert Kalish, Piano & Melodeon; with Robert Sheldon,
Flute & Keyed Bugle; Sonya Monosoff, Violin. Recorded with historical instruments at
the Smithsonian Institute, Washington, DC, Division of Musical Instruments.
Nonesuch Recordings H-71268 (Stereo), 1972.

Stephen Foster was an American composer of drawing-room ditties in the 1840s, '50s, and '60s, perhaps best known for 'Oh, Susannah', 'Camptown Races' and 'Old Folks at Home'. Although he lived his entire life in northern states, his work is associated with nostalgia for the old South, and some of his songs have had their lyrics shorn of racist references over the years.

I was not aware of this history when I listened to this album in childhood. The sleeve notes to the LP, recorded at the Smithsonian Institution in Washington, D.C., go no further than to say that 'his songs are, of course, period-pieces'. The artwork gives an impression of the sort of setting in which these songs would have been first enjoyed: an antebellum drawing room, with a dignified gent sporting a high collar and a thick mutton-chop beard leaning over three ladies in voluminous frocks who are concentrating on another lady in tulle playing a keyboard and singing.

The album came out of the sideboard on special occasions; it was not played as background music to our reading. Did we sing along? Unlikely: we would not have been so free and uninhibited, at least not my mother, my sister and myself. But the songs were of a type that my father would have enjoyed singing on a long car journey with all of us in tow, such as the annual trip to Kerry for our summer holiday, when he had a captive audience.

'There's a Good Time Coming', the second track on this album, is typical of the kind of song my father liked to sing: jaunty and upbeat, seemingly full of good humour despite its lyrics, which suggest a darker undertone of pathos. Here it is rendered by baritone Leslie Quinn along with Robert Sheldon on flute and Gilbert Kalish on piano:

> There's a good time coming, boys,
> A good time coming;
> We may not live to see the day,
> But Earth shall glisten in the ray,
> Of the good time coming.

I can imagine my father imitating this hearty baritone in his own, quite fine and deep singing voice. He liked songs with a strong narrative and tempo and good lyrics, his own repertoire extending to such songs as 'Poor Old Dicey Riley', and 'Down by the River Saile' and 'Johnson's Motor Car'.

The home, the homestead, is at the centre of Foster's songs, as one H. Wiley Hitchcock, Director of the Institute for Studies in American Music at Brooklyn College, points out in the record's extensive liner notes:

> It is worth recalling the function that such music had in American culture about the time of Foster. Composed neither for the recital platform nor the opera stage, it was aimed at the home – at the typical American parlour with its little square piano reed organ, its horse-hair-stuffed sofa, its kerosene lanterns, and candlelight.

Our 'parlour' consisted of a three-seater sofa and two armchairs, of foam rather than horse-hair; a side table; a seat on wheels we referred to as the 'pouf'; a fireplace; two bookshelves, one full-height, one half-height, both built by my father; and the stereo system on its own low shelving unit. Also rugs, cushions, paintings (many produced by my father), books, lamps, my mother's pottery, my father's cigar- and pipe-smoking paraphernalia, our cat, our dog, and us. My favourite at the time was 'Some Folks':

Some folks like to sigh,

Some folks do, some folks do;

Some folks like to die –

But that's not for me or you.

I misremembered this song for years, an alternative lyric running through my head that, interestingly, removes the mention of death:

Some folks like to cry,

Some folks do, some folks do;

Some folks like to sigh,

But that's not for me or you.

My own incorrect version is curiously apposite to my family, reflecting its active repression of emotional expression.

I who, I often felt when young, had reason to cry, never did so, not even on the occasion of my mother's hospitalizations for cancer treatment and her subsequent death in my late teens; I did not even cry at her funeral, but remained a mute, frozen, dumb thing throughout.

I had somehow learned not to cry. On one occasion, many years before my mother's death, aged nine or ten, the house full of agitation and disruption by visiting relatives, I was moved for the night from my bedroom to the room downstairs known as the study, where the piano and telephone were located, to sleep on a camp bed. Something unbeknownst to me was taking place, and there were numerous phone calls to the house during the night as I lay there trying to sleep, and people kept coming in and out of the room to receive them, disturbing me; the phone sat just above my head on a desk beside the camp bed.

At some point I became upset by all this disturbance, and cried out; finally, when my father came to check on me, he put his head around the door and did not come in to me but listened as I pleaded: 'The phone keeps ringing and they keep coming into the room to answer and wake me up.'

My father observed me coolly, where I was, in my pyjamas in the fold-out bed, distressed, and replied curtly, impatiently, dismissively. 'Stop being such a baby,' he probably said, or perhaps, even more characteristically, 'Stop your whingeing or I'll give you something to whinge about.'

Alone in the room facing him, I did not know where my mother was that night; it had been she I had wished to come to me when I cried out; I do not know why she did not come when I called. My father, summoned, had heard something in my tone, and had reacted to it by admonishing me to contain it; and I thus learned to do so.

To the child, all of this was unfair, untenable, unjust. Unjustifiable. Now, older than he was then, I want to place myself in my father's shoes. If I had but known at the time what was going on behind the scenes, I might have understood that my father was under duress; but I did not. Even now, I can merely guess: my mother, at a hospital, undergoing treatment for cancer, perhaps in a serious condition, the extended family up from the country to support my father, and someone staying overnight and so ousting me from my rightful place in my own bedroom. In the midst of this, the child crying out for his mother and pushing the father, already febrile with sadness and worry, over the edge so that he snaps, and speaks harshly to his son, silencing him, teaching him to keep his feelings to himself.

Foster's song echoed through my childhood; and I grew up a maudlin, repressed child, not able, or not willing, to express emotions, and always, always, mis-remembering those lyrics:

> Some folks like to cry,
> Some folks do, some folks do;
> Some folks like to sigh,
> But that's not for me or you.

4

Scott Joplin: 'Piano Rags by Scott Joplin': Joshua Rifkin, Piano: Nonesuch Records H-71248 (Stereo), 1970.

Scott Joplin was a Black American composer whose rags – syncopated piano instrumentals composed in the late nineteenth and early twentieth centuries – were rediscovered by audiences in the 1970s through Joshua Rifkind's best-selling recordings. This revival for ragtime reached its height at the time of the 1973 release of *The Sting*, starring Robert Redford and Paul Newman, which featured an adaptation of Joplin's 1902 rag 'The Entertainer'.

In the 1970 sleeve notes to his album *Piano Rags by Scott Joplin*, Rifkin notes:

> The awakening of interest in black culture and history during the last decade has not yet resurrected Joplin and his contemporaries, who remain barely known beyond a growing coterie of ragtime devotees. Yet it offers a perfect opportunity to discover the beauties of his music and accord him the honour he deserves.

Rifkin's intervention had the desired effect. At one point in the '70s it seemed everyone was listening to ragtime and attempting, at home, to play rags on piano or guitar.

I don't know exactly when my father bought this album, but I associate the music with my later childhood and adolescence, always there as a background, not least because we owned an upright piano, located in the study, on which I remember my sister trying to learn 'The Entertainer'. Although it starts with the challenge of a crescendo, this is a sedately-paced rag for the most part, and as such a good place to begin for those new to the form. My sister always managed to mess up the call-and-response structure of the chorus, hitting a wrong note at the same point every time. The sound of that duff note falling flat, but on tempo, will forever remain in my memory, as clear, if not more clear, than the correct note composed by Joplin himself; and later, when I attempted to learn the song on guitar, I fared little better than my sister had. Joplin's time structures and chording were fiendishly clever, complicated, sophisticated, and absolutely beautiful to hear when executed well.

It might just be the way I remember it now, but the '70s seemed an era of crazes. For example, 'spinners' became all the rage one summer; these were a type of yo-yo, and 'spinning' was the act of making the yo-yo body hover at the end of its string. From this starting point the spinner could be skimmed along the ground, or wrapped, still spinning, around limbs or objects.

All the kids had one, and all craved the skills to be good at spinning, and there were events organized to demonstrate such skills. So it was that one day there was much excitement and anticipation amongst us kids in the neighbourhood: a sponsor, probably one of the soft-drink companies whose labels appeared on the sides of our spinners, had arranged for a champion spinner to come to our neighbourhood corner shop to give a demonstration of his skills and the full range of the spinner's capabilities.

We all trooped up to the location, the shop at the side of the main road that had a small car park out front. The road was viciously busy and had few pedestrian crossings, but somehow we managed to cross en masse, and gathered gleefully in the car park, spilling out onto the pavement, cars whizzing past a few feet from where we stood.

Finally the champion, the pro, the spinning expert, arrived to give his demo. I recall him as a typical '70s man, stocky, with long fair hair that bounced when he moved, ginger sideburns, a too-tight T-shirt pulled over his bulging chest and arms, a gold medallion on a chain visible through the chest hair sprouting at his collar, and those nylon shorts with a slit on the side, which revealed far too much of his pale and bulging hairy legs and buttocks.

He gets out his spinner, and goes through with his demonstration; he is skilled, no doubt about it, but then it is not really very difficult to work a spinner, not if you are an adult who has practised. Nor, it turns out, is there much a spinner can actually do; quite rapidly the pro runs through all the tricks in his repertoire. There is a sense of urgency to this display; the pro, we feel, has been many places with this demo, and has many more to go to.

Then, because it is a promotion after all, and something must be promoted, we either buy, or are given, samples of a product; the details of this are lost to memory, but miniature sample-size cans of a soft drink come to mind. The kids, now full of sugary drink, become even more crazed. The crowd of us, gleeful and giddy, are in awe of the spinning champion: he appears, in his nylon shorts and with his hulking frame, to be a god amongst men. We can't get enough, and this seems to sum up the essence of a '70s craze: the product that has to be acquired, the illogical passion surrounding it, and the way it all disappeared into oblivion just as quickly as it appeared, only to be replaced by another, even more urgent and potent craze.

Other crazes included skateboards and, later, roller-boots. We took our skateboards to school and rode them home; we went to the roller-disco with our roller-boots. Or rather the other boys did. I did not possess a pair of roller-boots, as they were deemed too expensive, and did we not have a totally serviceable pair of roller-skates, formerly belonging to my sister, somewhere in the house, that I could use instead?

Roller-boots were cool; my sister's roller-skates were not. But not having any choice, I used the roller-skates, clumsy grey metal things with flimsy white leather straps, so as to have something to use when the other kids got into their shiny leather roller-boots. I was ridiculed for wearing them.

I preferred my skateboard anyway, which was navy, in a hard plastic, with thick vulcanized rubber wheels, and which I continued to use long after the skateboard craze was over; I think I went on spinning long after that craze was over too.

5

'Classical Japanese Koto Music': Izumi-Kai Original Instrumental Group.
An Everest Production, LA, Everest 3206, 1968.

The choice of what record to play in the living room was not subject to a democratic process; for the most part my father selected what was put on the stereo. This was tolerated by everyone else in the family. As I got older I would be allowed to slip on the occasional jazz album from my own modestly growing collection, usually a Blue Note or Vanguard re-release I would have bought with my pocket money in Murray's Record Centre, although I could not get away with anything too raucous.

Electric blues records – I had acquired a few Chess recordings in my early adolescence – were out of the question. 'That sounds like something her next door would put on,' my father would say sarcastically upon hearing the first chords of an Otis Rush or Howlin' Wolf song. 'Her next door' was a harmless lady from the Midlands who listened almost exclusively to Country and Western, which we could hear through the walls of our semi-detached house. She did at one point lend my mother some Dory Previn records, which my mother loved, and which I am now in possession of; presumably the neighbour did not think it appropriate to come ask for them back once my mother was diagnosed with, and then succumbed to, her illness, and no one in my family ever bothered to bring them back to her either.

My mother was also granted some leeway to play her Cleo Laine & John Williams record, and her Roger Whittaker disc; while my sister would occasionally put on *Jesus Christ Superstar* or *Sgt. Pepper's Lonely Hearts Club Band*, the latter a gift from my father's firm in return for some work-experience task she had done there. But mostly it was my father making the musical choices, leaving BBC Radio 3 running in the background on the radio during dinner, and putting records on later in the evening.

Sometimes my father seemed to hesitate when it came to choosing what to put on; and at such times, groaning inwardly, the rest of us would attempt to influence his decision: 'Not a plinky-plonk!' This phrase referred to my father's extensive collection of recordings of traditional music from around the world. My father adored this music – field and studio recordings from Africa and Asia for the most part. My father listened to these recordings in deep concentration, devoting his complete attention to whatever he had chosen to play, but we were not in any way attuned to their beauty and power.

These records came, for the most part, from a mail-order company in the UK, as they could not be got in stores in Ireland. The catalogues listing these records came from a neighbour down the road in our estate. This neighbour, a schoolteacher, who owned no car and cycled everywhere, put all the money thus saved into building his record collection, which was vast, filling shelf after shelf in a utility room devoted to its storage.

My father used to go to this neighbour's house to listen to his latest acquisitions and to check out his catalogues. The neighbour ordered albums from the mail-order company in bulk, simply ticking every box on every page and sending off for the lot. Huge packages of records would arrive for him at his house, and sit unopened for months, if not longer; he didn't have time to listen to all the records he ordered. My father ordered much more modestly, perhaps adding a choice or two of his own to be included in the neighbour's delivery to save postage costs.

Classical Japanese Koto Music, played by the Izumi-Kai Original Instrumental Group, comes in the form of a pristine Everest LP, the sleeve still wrapped in the cellophane it came delivered in, neatly cut by my father. The koto is a fretted stringed instrument, played with finger-picks; it is described on the sleeve notes to Everest 3206 as being 'the most important instrument of Japanese art-music'. In these recordings, the koto is accompanied by a haunting, swooping sound of the fuye, a Japanese flute, as well as the more piercing sound of the hichiriki, a sort of oboe.

My mother, my sister and I made it clear we did not enjoy this music, and as a child I heard it as vastly strange, off-putting, ugly and alien. But I like to think that there were moments when we became hypnotized by it too, drawn into its undoubted splendour, so that my father was not always left alone in his appreciation of it.

6

Richard Strauss, 'Also sprach Zarathustra': Herbert von Karajan, Conductor,
Berliner Philharmonic; Michel Schwabé, Solo-Violin;
Deutsche-Grammophon 4474322 (1974).

I have a clear memory of the opening movement of Richard Strauss's tone poem *Also sprach Zarathustra* as played on LP, reverentially, by my father. But this record is missing from the collection now in my possession.

The music, specifically the opening phrase, is most famous from its use in a key scene in Stanley Kubrick's film *2001*; and it's possible that a television viewing of this film in later years prompted my father's sudden interest in owning a recording of it. Certainly, he seemed unusually excited the day he brought home the record, and hurried us all to gather around the stereo to listen. He explained in doing so that we needed to pay attention to the famous opening, the orchestra barely audible at first, then building gradually and imperceptibly in increments to a crescendo of thundering percussion.

My father crouched down at the turntable and played the record and waited for a reaction. We were suitably impressed with the bombastic opening bars, our enthusiasm possibly bolstered by our awareness of the music from the film. But what then? The music continues for a good half-hour, and, in reality, nothing that follows quite matches that outstandingly dramatic opening.

Was my father disappointed by the rather mundane music that made up the bulk of *Also sprach Zarathustra*? Embarrassed even? It is difficult to say, because I seldom knew what he was feeling, unless it was anger.

I have a sense, too weak and faint to be fully recalled, that my father decided at that moment not to keep that record, but rather sheepishly returned it to its sleeve, the sleeve to the bag from where it was bought, and, at some later point, exchanged the record for another, if that was possible, or gave it away. That is the only explanation I can think of for the record's absence from the collection now in my possession; for the collection appears otherwise, to my memory, complete.

7

Johannes Brahms: Clarinet Quintet; Keith Purdy, Clarinet, Gabrieli Quartet;
EMI Classics for Pleasure CFP 152 (1970)

Wolfgang Amadeus Mozart, Carl Maria von Weber: Klarinettenkonzerte;
Heinrich Geuser, Klarinette, Radio-Symphonie-Orchester, Dirigent: Ferenc Fricsay,
Heliodor 89814, (19??).

Wolfgang Amadeus Mozart: Clarinet Quintet; Oboe Quartet: Gabrieli Quartet, Keith
Puddy (Clarinet), Jan Wilson (Oboe), EMI Classics for Pleasure CFP 121 (1970).

'How about a tootle on the flootle?' my father said often to me by way of encouragement, and, thus pressed, I would go, grudgingly, and practise my clarinet playing.

There was quite lot of clarinet music played in the house. As well as these recordings of Brahms, Weber and Mozart, I also had my own – now lost – Acker Bilk record, and I played his recordings of light classics and jazz frequently as a teenager, before I got into more serious jazz. Meanwhile, while still in primary school I had taken up the clarinet myself and started to study for grade exams.

My first lessons were in the evening in a music academy just a five-minute walk from where we lived. I bought my first clarinet, a wooden Yamaha model, through the school, taking so long to unwrap its several components from their cellophane wrappings that my music teacher, much to my annoyance, intervened and finished the task for me.

Becoming a clarinet player had been my father's idea, not my own, and I never warmed to the instrument. I found it difficult to form a decent embouchure in the lips and lacked the strength in my lungs to sustain the sheer blowing power required. I managed to make it to Grade 4 in my exams before more or less abandoning the instrument after I started college.

At that stage, the period when my mother was seriously ill, my father no longer seemed to care whether I played or not. Indeed, by then – aged in his early fifties, the age I am now – he hardly spoke to me at all, and I barely spoke to him.

Being able to play the clarinet meant that at times over the years I was called upon to play in public. Once I did so, with a small ensemble of other boys, at the funeral mass of a fellow secondary-school boy who had died. During this service we were placed on the altar to play, facing the front row; and there sat the boy's family, and I found their weeping and pain difficult to witness, perhaps in part because I was so used to keeping such emotions in check. Meanwhile, throughout the service, I bickered with the boy next to me, a tall youth with dark hair and spots, another clarinet player, who pointedly and stubbornly refused to offer me a replacement reed for my clarinet, as mine had split; I was painfully conscious of the notes my faulty reed was producing.

Much later – having, in my mind, given up on the clarinet – I played accompaniment to a musical staged by the university drama society. By that stage I preferred to belt out Bob Dylan and Neil Young songs to simple chord backing on my junk-store-bought acoustic guitar. But I was a regular in the Dramsoc, and once the director of the musical became aware that I could play clarinet, I was roped in to do so.

Every so often in later years I'd be struck by a wave of enthusiasm for the instrument, and so take it out and attempt once more, despite the passage of time and the erosion of memory of notes and notation, to play a formerly favourite piece of music by Brahms or Mozart, or perhaps Witold Lutosławski, whose challenging and piercing *Dance Preludes* I felt a particular affinity for although I never possessed a recording of them.

It was always my father who had encouraged me to play, wished me to play, the clarinet. He paid for the instrument, for the lessons; he paid for the Grade Examinations I took forever to pass; and he had reminded me to practise when otherwise I would have continued reading or making Airfix models: 'How about a tootle on the flootle?'

Did he really enjoy hearing me play from upstairs in my room, where I was struggling to produce a decent sound? He never said so. Still, my father encouraged me in his own clumsy way, unable to express in any other manner the pride he no doubt was feeling that his own son was attempting to play a classical instrument, and could read music, things he had never done, would never do.

Listening now to recordings of clarinet music by Brahms, Mozart and Weber, I am aware of how the instrument can sound when played by professionals, and I am reminded, ruefully, of what I do like about it – its sweet tone, fluency and voice – and I am tempted once more to pick it up, to try and play it again, even though I have a sense that it is now too late to do so.

8

'Africa: Ceremonial & Folk Music Recorded in Uganda, Kenya, and Tanzania by David Fanshawe', Nonesuch Records, H-72063, (1975).

'Ethiopia Vol 2: Music of the Desert Nomads: Jean Jenkins, Horniman Museum', Tangent Records, TGM 102 (Mono), (1970).

'Music of Africa Series Recorded by Hugh Tracey, No. 12, African Dances in the Witwatersrand Gold Mines Part 1', Decca, L032 (19??).

'Africa Shona Mbira Music Recorded in Mondoro & Highfields, Rhodesia, by Paul Berliner', Nonesuch Records, H-72077 (1977).

During the period when my father acquired these utterly beautiful recordings of traditional folk music from a number of countries in the African continent, the 1960s and '70s, there was an international folk music revival going on. The music of the Delta bluesmen of the 1930s was being rediscovered by collectors in the US, and there was an increasing interest in the traditional folk songs of Britain and Ireland. My father's interest in African music was taking place in parallel to this, and it appeared to be music that spoke to him at a deep level.

It is clear that, when these recordings were made, the ethnomusicologists who interpreted the music for listeners outside of Africa saw something transcendent in it. On the sleeve notes to *Africa: Ceremonial & Folk Music*, David Fanshawe writes of the 'thousand-mile journey in music' the music on the album represents. In the notes to the album *Music of the Desert Nomads*, the anonymous writer says: 'The music on this record has been selected partly for its beauty, and partly because it is representative of what may be heard in the great spaces of Ethiopia's deserts.' And in his notes for the album *Africa*

Shona Mbira Music, Paul Berliner writers of the sublime music contained therein: 'Listeners find the music has a powerful effect on them – it stimulates the imagination and makes them "think deeply".'

The albums offer only a tiny glimpse of the continent's vast range of musics, and I am left speculating as to what this music represented to my father, and how he valued it. Did he dream of that 'thousand-mile journey', he whose most distant travel experience was a brief business trip to Italy? Did he dream of escape, distant lands, or of experiencing such music in a live setting?

I did not think, as a child, to ask him what he dreamed of, or what he felt, as he listened to this music. But I like now to think of his placing an LP such as one of these on the turntable, setting it to play, sitting down to listen, and then settling in for a while to 'think deeply'.

9

Golden Guinea Series Volume 1: Rimsky-Korsakov: 'Scheherazade'; Tchaikovsky: 'Capriccio Italien', 'Swan Lake' (Extracts), '1812' Overture, 'Romeo and Juliet': The Nord Deutsches Symphony Orchestra conducted by Wilhelm Rohr; The London Philharmonic Orchestra Conducted by Sir Adrian Boult; PYE Golden Guinea GGD0089 (1961).

This anthology of classical romantic Russian music is billed on its sleeve as a 'Two-record Album Priced at only 32/6 Complete', thus placing it in the pre-decimal money era. The sleeve features an image of the Royal Festival Hall on the South Bank in London, extensive notes in its gatefold, and advertising on the reverse for other records in the series that mark it as of its era.

The sleeve notes state:

One need not necessarily be an avid lover of classical music to appreciate the music contained on this album. They are all works by the two great Russian composers Tchaikovsky and Rimsky-Korsakov, works that are known and loved by almost everybody, they will provide endless hours of enjoyment for you and your family for many years to come, an album to be treasured and played often.

This was my first record.

In the early 1970s, when we moved from Kerry to Dublin, a portable Bush Radio London Transistorised Record Player came with us. It was a black box with a steel-fronted grille containing its speaker, plugs for external connections on its leading edge, and internal volume and balancing knobs. When my father bought his first hifi system, consisting of separate components, several years later, he gave me the Bush portable, and along with it this record to play.

The portable Bush, which I had in my bedroom, allowed me to play a record on repeat, and I played this record over and over while I read in my room, under the blankets with a torch, late at night. I particularly remember reading and re-reading C.S. Lewis's *Narnia* series, seven books all told, as I listened to the strains of *Scheherazade* play from the mono portable in the corner of my bedroom.

Today the album, six decades old, produces not only the lyrical music of the Russian masters but also an alarming soundscape of pops, crackles and hisses. It is unlikely that as a child I cleaned the records contained in the set very often or diligently, and now the dust and dirt is firmly embedded in the grooves.

But still, under that patina of surface noise is the transcendent music of my first record, music that transports me always to the fantasy world I read about, and the real world that I was reading in: the world of my past, my childhood home, my childhood, my family, and, in particular, my father.

Notes on contributors

CAELAINN BRADLEY's first novel is to be published next year.

BRIAN DILLON's new book is *Suppose a Sentence*.

ARNOLD THOMAS FANNING is the author of *Mind on Fire: A Memoir of Madness and Recovery*.

SORCHA HAMILTON writes for the *Irish Times* and is working on a novel.

JANE LAVELLE is working on a collection of short stories.

LIA MILLS's most recent novel is *Fallen*.